KV-052-135

DEDICATION

To my mother,
who understood all young people so well

ACKNOWLEDGEMENTS

Great thanks to Fiona Brennan whose hilarious revelations about life as a teenager were so very helpful.

And thanks to Niamh—whose cheer was more encouraging than she'll ever know

And a depth of gratitude too to Cissie Brady, an inspirational lover of life for eighty-four years, for her memories.

ABOUT THE AUTHOR

Rose Doyle, bestselling author of *Images* and *Tarantula*, a book for children, lives in Sandymount, Dublin. She has two young sons.

The swallows are making them ready to fly,
Wheeling out on a windy sky:
Goodbye, Summer, goodbye, goodbye.

From 'Goodbye, Summer' by G. J. Whyte-Melville
(1821–1878)

CHAPTER ONE

The train journey was a nightmare. The view, of twinkling waves under a beaming sky, was a grotesque mockery of the way I was feeling. If it hadn't been for my insatiable optimism I'd have pulled the cord and leaped into the blue at Killiney.

Instead I sat on, sweltering in my seat, senses assaulted on every side. The train was crowded with sweaty bodies headed for the port of Rosslare. From there they would sail on to holidays in France. And every hot, noisy and odiously cheerful one of them wanted to go where they were going. I was sure of it.

The train was taking me to the last place on earth I wanted to spend the summer I was sixteen.

I would be getting out at Wexford. From there I would be taken to a desolate headland called Keshkorran for a 'holiday' in the ancient hotel owned by my grandmother. I could only vaguely remember draughty old Lir House. My grandmother I couldn't remember at all. I had last seen her when I was four years old.

The fact that I so passionately didn't want to go to Lir House that summer makes you wonder about the role of fate in life. Because if I'd done what I wanted to do, which was spend time with man-of-my-dreams Manus while working on a million reasons why I shouldn't go back to school in September, I'd have missed the events that changed my life.

Nor that there was much chance of my being

allowed to doss about for the holidays. I was on the train within twenty-four hours of the arrival of a letter from my grandmother asking if I could spend the summer helping with the hotel's last season.

From the way my mother behaved you would think the request for a hotel skivvy was a heaven-sent solution to the problem of 'what to do with Martha for the summer'. 'You'll enjoy it down there,' she said firmly, standing in the door of my bedroom, the letter in her hand. When I looked at her incredulously she attempted an encouraging smile. This was not a success. Encouraging smiles are not part of my mother's range of expressions.

'I will not enjoy it! How could you even imagine I would! It's like sending me into exile.' I pulled the duvet over my head and turned to the wall.

'Don't be ridiculous, Martha.' I could tell from her voice that the bright smile had vanished. It was deadly quiet, with a touch of ice. An ominous sign. It meant she was determined to have her way. 'Take that cover off your head, please, and sit up. I want to talk to you.'

I sat up. It was the quickest way to get rid of her. I put on my stony face and looked straight ahead. This brought her across the room to stand in front of me. I managed, without moving my eyes, to focus on her midriff. She was dressed for work, wearing one of her impeccable navy-blue suits. My mother is impeccable even when she does the garden. She is small and neatly built. I am huge and awkward. We have nothing in common.

'Your attitude makes rational discussion impossible,' she went on in the icy voice. 'Therefore I'm going to make this decision for you.' (So, I thought, what's new? I said nothing.) 'I think it will be good for you to get out of Dublin for the summer. It will give you time to think things over, distance you a bit from…Manus.' She is so impossibly uptight about Manus that she had difficulty getting his name out. My lips must have tightened or something because she rushed through the rest of the 'discussion'.

'It's for your own good, Martha, believe me.' Do parents learn this phrase on the birth of their children? I sighed heavily and she waved the letter. 'A change of environment and some time on your own will help you come to your senses about going back to school. *And* about this photography business.' I turned and looked out of the window. The sun was shining, little birds were twittering. 'And I hope you will treat your grandmother with more respect than you do me.'

This made me turn to give her The Look. My mother had ignored her mother, the very grandmother I was now being asked to respect, for years. The Look combines disgust with disbelief. I have perfected it over the last three years or so. Ever since my mother and I began to have problems in fact. It made her flush bit but she hardly slowed down at all.

'And I *don't* want you calling Manus Byrne from Lir House. Apart from anything else, think of your grandmother's phone bill.'

This was rich, coming from someone who hadn't given a toss about grandmother's bill, or anything else about her, for years. I said nothing, just continued to give her The Look. For once she didn't come up with her usual, 'Take that expression off your face, madam, when I'm talking to you.' She obviously didn't care to hear what I was thinking.

'I'll ring your grandmother and tell her to expect you tomorrow. That will give you today to get packed. And Martha…' She paused meaningfully, 'I've already discussed this with your father and he agrees with me. So there's no point in your appealing to him.'

I knew that anyway. Dad always agrees with her. He doesn't like hassle and sort of drifts away when my mother starts on me. He hasn't backed me up once in three years. I don't really know why my mother started ripping into me for every little thing when I got to thirteen but I do know that the complaints and nagging since then have been never ending. She expects the worst all the time and is surprised when she doesn't get it.

'I'm sure you've covered all the angles,' I said bitterly. Then I yawned. 'Can I go back to sleep now?' We were both equally fed up. But she only had herself to blame. She left the room without another word.

Just a minute and a half later, the time it took to collect her navy-blue handbag from the kitchen table, the front door banged behind my mother. Then the car backed out and she was gone. Nothing ever upsets my mother's routine. Certainly not her only daughter's depression. But then she had no idea, no idea at all, of the misery I felt . If she did she wouldn't, couldn't, have been so cruel as to separate me from the boy I loved, and from all my friends, for two and a half months.

There was also the little matter of her denying me the right to pursue the career in photography I'd my heart set on. And her determination that I would 'complete' my education. The birds twittered on outside. I pulled the duvet over my head again. It was as if my life had ended for the summer, so deprived of meaning had it become.

Sleep proved impossible. I got out of bed and phoned my friend Naomi Ingles. She's been my confidante since I was eleven. She is also unlike me in every way, being hyper and competitive and very keen about 'getting on'. Naomi, as well as having a pretty name, is petite, has a lovely face and a really nice mother. Most days my face looks as if it hasn't decided what it's going to do with itself yet. What Naomi and I have in common these days is mainly the fact that we know each other a long time.

She didn't immediately grasp the awfulness of what had happened. 'Looks like being a pretty dead summer around here anyway.' She sounded sleepy.

'Naomi, did you *hear* what I said?' I practically screeched down the phone. 'I'm being packed off to red-neck country.'

'But it's not for ever, is it?'

She sounded only half-awake so I explained further.

'It might as well be. I'm to be buried on the top of a cliff for the entire summer. I'm to skivvy for an old woman I don't even know in a house that's probably falling down. And I won't see Manus for two months or more.'

'I'll look after him for you.'

'Thanks a lot, for nothing.'

It wasn't that I didn't trust Naomi. She was, after all, my best friend. Plus there was the added safeguard that Manus didn't like her. He thought her pushy. What was far more likely was that someone else would muscle in. I wasn't the only female to find Manus Byrne attractive.

5

'Oh, come on Martha! Get a grip.' Naomi yawned again, loudly. She gets bored easily. 'Look, I'll call round to you. And I'll lend you my American back-pack to put your things in. See you in an hour or so.'

I didn't want her sodding back-pack. While I waited for her I dressed and tried to get my head around what was happening to me.

The arrival of the letter was, in itself, surprising. I am called after my grandmother but as far as I was concerned she could have kept the one thing she'd ever given me. Martha is not exactly a name to set hearts dancing or bells ringing. Coupled with Hayes it's a lead weight.

Downstairs, ignoring the muesli my mother had pointedly left on the kitchen table, I made myself a breakfast of toast with hot chocolate. As I emptied the her bowl of roughage into the bin I wondered, for the first time, about my mother's relationship with my grandmother. To ask her about it now, when things between us were at an all-time low, did *not* seem a good idea. If it was a case of history repeating itself then I just didn't want to know.

I tried instead to remember my grandmother. All I managed was a blurry image of a tall woman leaning over me and smelling of flowers. I tried to remember Lir House, too, but big and dark was all that came to mind. Both memories were probably my imagination.

My grandmother had never visited us in Dublin. I can't say I blame her. We are an extraordinarily dull family and have very few visitors anyway. My mother likes us to 'keep ourselves to ourselves'; exactly why, I've never been able to fathom. My father is an accountant. My brother Garret, two years older than me, plans to go into his office. My mother, when she's not looking for dusty corners to clean, works in an insurance office. Our grass is the shortest on the road, our windows the shiniest. We bore me to death. The year before I had announced to the household my intention of becoming a photographer. The news failed to impress. That Saturday afternoon's frenzy of dusting, clipping and car-washing went on as if I hadn't spoken. Since then I have consistently failed to excite their interest in my career choice. It's not as if I wanted to do something disgraceful. All I want to do is take pictures that catch for ever something special about events or people. They don't have to be pictures of important people or even of big events, just so long as they say something and make people really look. A job as a press photographer would suit me just fine.

Reaction has been livelier to my desire not to return to school in September. Despite my turning in less than brilliant reports the response has been a resounding 'no' from both parents. I think they actually agree on that one. But I haven't abandoned the battle, on either front.

Manus Byrne has also caused much negative reaction *en famille*. They said I was too serious about him. He's eighteen, with dark hair and blue eyes. Also he's taller than me. When you're five feet nine inches and towering over most people your own age, this is not unimportant. At school I was called Big Bird to my face. I don't want to know what I was called behind my back.

Manus came into my life around Easter time, just after I'd dispensed with train-tracks on my teeth. I'm a feminist, of course, and really had no interest in boys before that. But Manus was just irresistible.

If my mother imagined that I would forget him in the excitement of skivvying in Lir House then she was mistaken. I would not forget him. I would never forget him.

CHAPTER TWO

I knew, getting on the train next morning, that the journey was going to be a nightmare. My mother, wearing her long-suffering face, drove me to the station.

Along with my own pretty sour expression I was wearing a black T-shirt. I was in mourning for my life.

'You're to wait at the station in Wexford until someone arrives to collect you,' my mother said, presenting me with my return ticket. I shrugged and took it from her.

'I'm hardly likely to start hawking my bags along country roads,' I said.

Into two bags, one of them Naomi's, I had packed my camera, which was a modest 35-mm Pentax with a 70-S zoom. I'd bought it second-hand with the money I'd got for my sixteenth birthday. Along with it I had packed generous rations of books and clothes. I'd been unable to make up my mind about the clothes, so had packed almost every stitch I owned.

My mother carefully checked her change and we slipped into the stream of people making for Platform 5. The train was late. Trains, in my experience, are always late. My mother, unable to accept this reality, began an agitated dance, shifting from one foot to the other as she eyed the station clock. 'I'm going to be really late for work at this rate,' she fussed.

'There's no need for you to wait with me,' I said coldly. I knew quite well she would stick around until I was safely locked into a moving carriage.

I ignored her waving figure as the train pulled out but took last, long looks at dear, dishevelled Dublin as we crossed the Liffey. There was a lump in my throat and it was an effort not to cry.

But I had one golden and consoling secret. Manus, on the phone the night before, had promised to come down to Lir House to see me. He hadn't said when but just knowing he would arrive some time was good enough for me. I hugged the prospect to myself as we rattled out along Dublin Bay.

It had been an amazingly hot, dry summer so far. As they fell behind us, the suburbs, and civilisation, were baking lazily in the sun.

That was when I started to feel suicidal. I was a true child of the city. Town life was what I understood. I liked to feel a part of things, to know what was going on. But I didn't jump and, as the train made its hot and sticky way down the coast, I was figuring out how old my grandmother might be.

My mother, I knew, was forty-five. I knew this because of a decline she'd gone into around the time of her forty-fifth birthday in April. For once I'd felt some sympathy for her. I can just about imagine being twenty. Forty-five must be like approaching death's door. No wonder she'd been depressed. She'd gone on for weeks about being aware of her own mortality and wanting to do something with her life.

Hearing her talk like that had surprised me. Realising that she expected me to understand, and help, had surprised me even more. Anyway, I had enough problems of my own. And she was the cause of too many of them. In the end my mother got over her age crisis without help. And without making any changes, that I could see, in her life or attitudes.

While I was thinking about all of this my grandmother's age came to me. I remembered my mother, during her age crisis, going on a bit about my grandmother. At one point she had moaned on about her becoming 'both a mother and a widow when she was twenty-nine'.

I remembered it because it meant, of course, that my mother couldn't have known her father. I'd known he was dead a long time, but not that he'd died when she was a baby. A little simple addition gave me my grandmother's age. She was seventy-four.

I wondered if I could get her to tell me about my dead grandfather over the summer. It would be interesting, but I wasn't hopeful. Given that she'd ignored me for years, and had written now only because she wanted cheap labour, she was hardly likely to be the type who went in for cosy reminiscences.

We stopped at a one-horse station. I missed the name and realised I didn't have a notion where we were. I kept my eye peeled for the sign at the next station and discovered we'd reached Wicklow. After that we went inland a bit, through a sea of green woods. It was all so petrifyingly picturesque that it put me to sleep. I awoke when the old man beside me poked me in the ribs. He was pointing to a wide river, low because of the fine weather.

'Used to poach salmon there,' he chortled, 'and eat them raw, almost. We used to light fires on the bank and give them a bit of a turn.'

I said nothing. I didn't want to encourage him. I looked at the river. Six swans cruised down the centre. They were replaced, as the train swept on, by views of a round tower, some boats, rows of sheds, much flowering greenery and, slowly and at last, by a crowd of Japanese tourists on a platform.

We had arrived in Wexford.

No one was waiting for me. Not a granny, not a hotel porter—that would have been a laugh—no one. I got off and stood, patiently tapping my foot, while the Japanese disappeared into the train. It moved off and I was alone on the platform with nothing to do but admire the station's blue and orangey-pink paintwork. This became a bit sickening after a while so I picked up my bags. It was time to venture into whatever awaited beyond the station.

Immediately outside there was a square with grass in the middle and a monument. I wandered over and sat at its base, saw it was dedicated to one John Edward Redmond. The name brought memories of history classes and, despite the heat of the sun, I shivered.

I put all this out of my mind and leaned back against John Redmond's monument to wait for whomever, or whatever, was to come. It was quite nice there, with people walking about and the buzz of traffic in the background. I began a little day-dream about Manus.

'Put this on!'

I heard the voice and saw the helmet at the same time but didn't connect them with me. Not even when the helmet waved in front of my eyes and the voice, more loudly, said again, 'Put this on!'

Its owner had to crouch down and snap his fingers before it registered. 'Wakey, wakey!' he said. 'I'm the transport to Lir House. Only you can't travel unless you wear a helmet. Here.' He dropped the helmet into my lap and stood up. I got to my feet too and squinted up at him. He was quite tall, at least two inches taller than me, and thin. More than that it was difficult to see since he wore a helmet himself.

He picked up one of my bags and walked toward a parked motorbike. I put on the head gear, picked up the other bag and followed him. This was not what I'd expected. My grandmother in a model-T Ford would have been more believable somehow. The last of the great romantics, that's me.

My Mr Charming was revving the bike when I got there. 'Helmet feel all right?' he asked and I nodded. It didn't come off.

I got on behind the bag he'd already loaded on to the bike and hung the other across my back. I'd hardly balanced myself before he moved off, fast.

I'd a strange sense of *déjà-vu* as we went through Wexford town. I kept imagining I could remember the narrow streets, their strange twists and hilly turns. Then we were clear of the town and going fast along a wide, busy road.

'How far is it?' I yelled after a few minutes.

'Not far.' He waved an arm but didn't seem inclined to say more.

It was a heavy bike and we fairly thundered along before turning to rocket up a steep, high-hedged road, almost vertically uphill, until the sea came into view again and the road turned sharply into a pair of high, stone-pillared gates. We sped along a wide and bumpy avenue, hardly slowing down at all. I wasn't feeling very secure and things didn't improve when we hit an expanse of gravel.

But this, at last, slowed us down and allowed me to grab my first look at Lir House. A long, ivy-covered mass registered before my driver did a quick, gravel-spinning U-turn and faced us back the way we'd come.

He stopped, lifted my bag and dumped it on the ground. 'Hold on to the helmet for me,' he said as I followed the bag. 'I'll collect it when I come to work later.' He revved the engine and I moved away from the shooting gravel. 'I'm Lorcan O'Neill,' he yelled. 'See you around.'

He went then, much too fast along the bumpy avenue. I wondered if he was in a hurry somewhere or just showing off. I decided it was the latter. I turned to look at the house again. A figure moved out of the front door and stood, in the shadow of the portico, waiting. I took off the helmet and began walking toward my grandmother.

CHAPTER THREE

I walked slowly, taking in Lir House as I went. It was smaller than I'd expected. But it was still a big house, droopy and tired in the sunshine. The walls looked as if they were held up by the ivy which covered them and the long windows yawned open. So did the faded yellow door, in front of which my grandmother stood waiting.

She was dressed in black and white and was so still she looked like an old photograph. As I came closer she moved down on to the gravel. She stood quite still again but I could see now that she was smiling.

This encouraged me and I covered the last few yards quite quickly.

'Martha!' She held out her hands. 'Here at last!' Her voice was deep and rusty-sounding, like someone who smoked a lot of cigarettes. Up close she was not at all what I'd imagined from a distance and I tried not to stare as I stood in front of her.

She was tall and thin with a face of the craggy, lined variety. She had an immense amount of untidy, whitey-yellow hair and grey eyes which looked and at me with frank curiosity. Up close, the black-and-white outfit was a fairly bedraggled affair too.

I dropped the bag I was holding and held out a hand. To save my life I couldn't have grabbed both her hands, though that was obviously what she expected me to do. She pumped my hand up and down, her grip surprisingly strong. 'What a grand big girl you are.'

I could have lived without hearing this and bristled a bit. She gave a dark chortle and looked at me even more closely. 'The train was packed.' I'm not usually so inane but the staring and hand-shaking was making me uncomfortable.

'I'm sure it was,' my grandmother said. 'I'm sure it was. Always is, in the summer. Well, well...'

She seemed as stuck for words as I was myself. As I racked my brain for some remark she pulled me close and gave me a quick, hard hug. I got a dizzying whiff of flowery perfume and the brief feel of a bony chest. Before letting me go she planted a dry, feathery kiss on my cheek.

I should have returned the kiss but I hesitated and the moment passed. I might have been facing a perfect stranger. She was simply an old woman I did not know. But how could I? And how could she know me? In the twelve years since we'd last met I'd grown up and she'd grown old.

She nodded at the helmet I was still holding in my hand. 'I hope Lorcan didn't keep you waiting,' she said. 'He's a decent lad. Good cook too. He's looking after the kitchen for the summer so you'll be well fed anyway. I'm sure you could do with a bite to eat right now. Come on inside.'

I picked up my bag and followed her. As we stepped under the portico a large, grey cat sidled out the front door. My grandmother stopped and made a tut-tutting noise, which he completely ignored. I knew immediately that he was a tom; he had that fat, complacent look. I like cats but from the very beginning my grandmother's gave me the creeps. I never, ever, saw what she saw in him. That first day, when she attempted to pick him up, he side-stepped her and jumped out on to the gravel. Sitting there he looked straight back at me with cold, unblinking eyes, his tail moving like a slow brush over the pebbles.

'Fiachra's the best mouse-catcher I've ever had,' my grandmother said, 'but he's not very sociable. Give him a day or two.'

I had another attack of *déjà vu*, like the one I'd experienced coming through Wexford town, as I stepped over the threshold and into the hallway of Lir House.

It was dark after the sun outside. Apart from the door the only other light came from a window over the turn on the stairs. I stood blinking as my eyes adjusted and knew that I had stood there before doing the same thing. I knew too what I would see when my vision cleared. The staircase ahead was wide, as I'd expected, and there was dark wood everywhere. Someone had attempted to cheer things up by putting a great vase of rhododendrons and cow-daisies on a table. There was a telephone and notebook on the table too.

'You can leave your things here.' My grandmother waved a vague hand and continued on toward a door at the back of the hallway. I did as she suggested, followed her and found myself in the kitchen.

With a long finger my grandmother indicated that I should sit at the table. 'Lorcan's left something here for your lunch.'

I pulled out a wooden chair and sat down. It was bright in the kitchen and as she fussed about I had another look at her. A shoulder pad in her black cardigan had come loose and fallen down the sleeve. It made her look like a lopsided woman with a lumpy arm. She really did have a lot of hair too. She had attempted to catch it up with combs over each ear but wisps and whole clumps had escaped. The combs, mother-of-pearl, were very pretty.

She turned quickly from the fridge and caught me, bang on, as I gave her the old scrutiny. 'Well,' she said with a smile, 'am I everything a grandmother should be?'

I refused to be embarrassed. Why shouldn't I be curious? 'You're the only one I have so I wouldn't know,' I said. Which was true—Dad's parents died when I was young. My grandmother laughed and her face cracked into a zillion wrinkles.

'Well, that simplifies matters,' she said, 'and makes us even, since you're the only grandchild I'm likely to meet. We can both start from scratch.'

While I tried to figure out this remark, wondering how she could be so sure she would never meet Garret, my grandmother held up a plate of salad. My heart fell. I was much more than salad-hungry. I'd refused both breakfast (meusli again) and the sandwiches my mother had made for me to take on the train. I'd no regrets of course, but the prospect of a salad did bring the ham and tomato sandwiches to mind.

Something of what I was thinking must have shown on my face because my grandmother quickly returned the salad to the fridge. 'You're hungry.' She took a soup tureen from the fridge and placed it on the table with a bowl. 'Have some of this while I make you a nice big omelette.'

I watched in disbelief as she ladled a greeny sludge into the bowl. I tried to stop it but my nose sniffed, loudly.

'Lorcan tells me it's iced apple soup,' my grandmother went on, filling the bowl. 'He likes to experiment. Try it.'

She pushed the soup in front of me, watching until I lifted the spoon and dipped it into it. She nodded encouragingly as, very slowly, I brought it to my mouth and tasted. It wasn't bad at all, as far as taste went anyway. As well as the apples, Chef Lorcan had used cream and some curry powder. I nodded and, apparently satisfied, my grandmother put on a vast, candy-striped apron.

I finished the soup without looking at it once. Instead I studied the kitchen. It was big, in ye olde style, and had seen better days. There were a great many wooden shelves and cupboards and a wide window looked on to the back garden. The cooker, sink and fridge looked post-war, but only just. An open fire was laid with logs and it was easy to imagine my grandmother sitting in the low armchair beside it in the wintertime. The table I sat at was of scrubbed wood.

I was aware of my grandmother cracking what sounded like a half-dozen eggs. As the omelette cooked she sat opposite me at the table.

'Now then, Martha,' she said, very businesslike, 'what are you going to call me?'

She fixed me with a long, grey gaze which I returned in some confusion. It sounded like a trick question, a test of some kind. Or maybe it was a joke. By way of avoiding the issue I tried a little half-baked wit. 'How about Nanny? Nana? Gransie?'

She frowned and shook her head. She was serious. 'I

don't think so.' She drummed skinny, white fingers on the table, thinking. It occurred to me that, as part of her labour force, she might expect me to call her Ma'am. Or something equally nonsensical.

'I've never been a one for titles,' she continued, 'but for you to call me Martha would be confusing, now that there are two of us around the place. I could live with being called Grandmother for the summer, however, if you could. What do you think?'

Smiling, she went back to the omelette, tipped it on to a plate and put it in front of me. I felt a pang of remorse for having suspected her of other intentions and was positively chirpy as I dug into the omelette.

'Grandmother's fine by me. I'd probably have called you that anyway. This is a great omelette, grandmother.' It was too. She watched as I ate. I didn't mind. I satisfied my great hunger before asking the question that was on my mind.

'What sort of things will you want me to help with for the summer, Grandmother?' It seemed to me better to get my job definition sorted out at the very beginning.

'Oh, I'll find something for you to do.' She sounded vague. 'I'm not expecting to be overcrowded this summer. You'll find the hours good. Plenty of time off.' She stood up, gave a wrinkly smile. 'Think I'll have some lunch myself.' She crossed to the fridge, came back with a can of Guinness, a glass and some cheese. She sat opposite me again, poured the Guinness, carefully, and took a long drink.

'Is your mother well?' She asked the question abruptly. My mouth was full at the time so I nodded. 'And your father? And brother? 'I nodded again, twice.

This seemed to satisfy her and she changed the subject. Much as I wanted to know about herself and my mother, I was relieved. I didn't want to know just yet.

'Now then, Martha,' she pleated her face into another smile, 'tell me what you're interested in.'

'Photography'.

'What kind of photography?'

'Oh, anything with a bit of life in it.'

'Anything with a bit of life in it. Indeed. ' She cut up a piece of cheese in silence before she looked at me and said, 'What is that supposed to mean?'

She made me feel a bit of a spoof, as if I didn't know what I was talking about. I wouldn't want anyone to think I was a spoof about photography so to put her right I began to explain about the kind of pictures I like to take, about the buzz I get from capturing those seconds that scream 'life' at you. It can be anything—a laughing or crying face, a child running, a dog scratching. At first my grandmother just went on eating, nodding a little, but then she stopped and really began to listen to me. She asked a few questions and even though she obviously knew nothing at all about photography she seemed to understand what I was talking about.

'What does your mother think of all this?' she asked eventually.

'Not much.' My mother's opinion was not something I wanted to get into.

'Didn't think she would.' She stood up. 'Well then, are you finished eating?'

I was. As I washed my plate—my mother's training in these matters is rigorous—I looked out at the back garden. It was sad, wildly overgrown and full of moribund fruit trees.

'I couldn't keep it up.' My grandmother, at my elbow, was matter of fact. 'Pity really. Come on now, I'll show you to your room.'

In the hallway I picked up my bags, leaving the helmet where it was, and followed her up the stairs. She stopped, puffing a bit, when we arrived on the first-floor corridor.

'These are the only bedrooms I use now.' Her voice was raspy. 'I've closed off the second floor. This will be your room.' She opened the nearest door, which was the second on the corridor. 'You'll be quite independent here.'

I stepped inside and saw what she meant. It was a bedroom made to be lived in. A wing-backed armchair stood by a long window with a view over the cliff-top and the sea beyond. There was a fireplace, a roll-top desk with another bunch of rhododenderons on top, some bookshelves and a gigantic old wardrobe. And there was a bed, also large and old.

I dropped my bags and bounced on it a bit, trying it for size and looking around as I did so. 'I like the room,' I said. 'It's three times as big as the one I have at home.'

'It was your mother's. Why don't you unpack and have a look at the rest of the house? I'll be downstairs if you need me.'

My grandmother pulled the door gently behind her as she left. I sat still, staring at its dark wood. A sort of shock tremor went through me. If she'd said the room was haunted I couldn't have been more taken aback. In a way, of course, that was exactly what she had said. I knew so little about my mother's life before me that it was like being thrust suddenly into the room, and life, of a long-ago stranger.

I got off the bed. Beds, according to my mother, the woman that stranger had become, were for sleeping in. I stood, looking round and trying to fit her into the room. I couldn't. No more than I could fit her into Lir House or see her as the daughter of the woman I was going to call 'Grandmother' for the rest of the summer.

I didn't feel like unpacking. My mother would have expected me to and I was tired of responding like a robot. Instead, I sat in the armchair by the open window. Ivy snaked along the sides and, in places, came almost into the room. I hoped it wasn't full of creepy-crawlies. Creepy-crawlies are one of the things I hate about the country. I looked down, into the garden. A path, overgrown but clear enough, led through it right to the edge of the cliff.

I sat there for ages and in all that time I saw no one, not a single human being. There was a deafening amount of noise; birds chirruping, bees buzzing and a dog, somewhere, barking. But there was not a sight or sound of anything human, anywhere on the headland.

It was terribly, shockingly, lonely.

I cried then, now that there was no one to see. I pulled my knees up, locked my arms around them and cried and cried. They were the first tears I'd allowed myself since my mother had announced I was being packed off. This was the reality. This lonely, decaying house, those noisy birds. And I was stuck here for the rest of the summer. Anger had kept me going until then, anger and the knowledge that Manus would be coming to see me. But even that prospect, right then, seemed poor consolation.

Basically, I'm a practical person. After a while my habit of making plans asserted itself and the tears stopped of their own accord. It's hard to plan and cry at the same time. I counted the plusses. My grandmother seemed all right, so far. Lorcan O'Neill might be an ally. Or he might be a perfect pain. I would have to suss him out over the next few days. Then there was the sea, blue and waiting for me to improve my breast stroke. I might even get the tan I hadn't managed to get in Dublin. And, of course, I had my camera. I took it out of the bag, placed it carefully on the desk. Just seeing it there made me feel better.

I unpacked then, deciding it was as well to get it over with. Stuffing things into the wardrobe, I wondered about the guests, why I hadn't seen any. They'd probably taken themselves off to enjoy the afternoon sun on a nearby beach. Lir House didn't appear to be awash with leisure facilities.

As I was closing the wardrobe door I had an unfortunate sighting of my hair in the mirror. It was short, neat and hateful. The cut, you couldn't call it a style, had nothing to do with me and everything to do with my mother's insistence that heavy hair like mine needed to be 'kept under control'. Well, she wasn't here and it could grow to my toes for all I cared. I would not let a sissors near it until September! I chalked this decision up as another plus and left the bedroom to explore.

In the corridor I stood a while, listening to the quiet of the house. When it became too much I counted the doors to either side of me. There were six. Since I occupied one and my grandmother, presumably, slept in another that left only four for guests.

I mooched along the corridor, opening the doors as I went. The room next to mine, smelling of her flowery perfume and with the surly Fiachra asleep on the bed, was obviously my grandmother's. Only one other, at the far end of the corridor, showed signs of occupation. As my grandmother had said, it didn't look as if I were going to be overworked.

I went downstairs and mooched around a bit more. There was a lot of heavy old furniture everywhere but it seemed to me that only two rooms, both of them to the front of the house, were in use. One, a dining room, had a long oval table with silver candlesticks. The other was a drawing room or library. It had two long windows on to the gardens and faded curtains which looked weighty and important. There were several old, well-stuffed armchairs and shelves and shelves of books. I liked it. It was relaxed, in an old-fashioned way.

But there was no TV anywhere. Or video. I couldn't believe it but decided not to think about the consequences, yet. The only photographs I came across were in this room. There were two of them, both of my mother and both in silver frames. In one she was about ten years old, wearing a serious smile and with her hair in a long plait. The other was a wedding picture I'd seen before. There were no photographs of my grandmother, nor of my grandfather. Not even the usual wedding snap.

Maybe my grandmother couldn't bear the sadness of being reminded of him. Or maybe there was something that made my grandfather better forgotten. Maybe he had shot himself. Or died from some socially unacceptable disease like AIDS or whatever the equivalent of the time had been. That would certainly be a skeleton to keep locked in the family cupboard. Maybe whatever it was had something to do too with the falling out between my mother and grandmother.

Finding out might be fun.

CHAPTER FOUR

I was poking through the books, which were mostly novels and poetry and gave no clues at all about the family history, when a car drove up the avenue.

I watched from the window as it crunched slowly across the gravel, almost to the window. A man got out, rushed round to open the other door and waited while a woman pulled herself from the passenger seat. She was a colossus on legs. I'd never seen anyone so fat.

Nor so entirely irritable looking. The man tried to take her arm as they began toward the house but she shook him off with a tremendous heave. He went on fussing and buzzing around her, like an agitated fly, as she stomped into the hall and out of my view. Seconds later the drawing room door was thrown open and the man's face bobbed anxiously round it. He blinked and withdrew when he saw me but then bobbed back again quickly, the whole of him this time.

'Do you mind if my wife and I join you?' he asked.

His accent sounded Scottish. He was wearing a yellow shirt and his neck and arms were a roaring red from the sun. Before I could answer, the fat woman, gasping and puffing, pushed past him into the room.

'It's the greenhouse effect.' She lowered herself into an armchair. 'We're all going to be fried alive before the end of the century. You mark my words.' Her accent was definitely Scottish.

'Now, now, my love.' The man fixed a cushion

behind her back. 'Don't depress the lass. She's only starting out in life. She doesn't want the worry of things like that.'

'She *should* be worrying about things like that.' The woman glared at me from eyes that were almost buried in folds of flesh. 'It's no good just some of us worrying ourselves sick about it. We all have to do our bit.'

'I'm sure the lass does what she can.' The man nodded at me and I nodded back. His wife wasn't the kind of person you willingly antagonised.

'Didn't see you here this morning,' she said then, 'nor last night either. Are you here with your parents?'

'I'm here to—'

'Take my advice.' The woman leaned forward and interrupted in a loud whisper. 'Book a night at a time. I'm not sure that this place is up to the mark. Not sure at all. It depends what you're used to, of course.' She sank back into the chair and shook with a great sigh. 'See if you can get me a whiskey and soda, Ron, will you? That's if there's such a thing as service in this place.'

She closed her eyes and Ron jumped up. I scuttled into action myself and got to the door before him. 'I'll get it,' I said. 'I'm working here for the summer.'

A quiver of flesh, followed by a thin, dark glitter, indicated that the woman's eyes had opened. 'Ice,' she snapped. 'And plenty of it.'

In the hallway I almost collided with my grandmother. She was on her way up from the kitchen and was wearing a black velvet beret into which she'd miraculously tucked all her hair. 'I see you've met Ron and Mabel,' she said.

'How long will they be staying?' It was the first

thing which came into my head. The thought of having the fat woman around the place for weeks depressed me far more than the prospect of an overheated planet.

'Not long.' My grandmother took my arm and turned back toward the kitchen with me. 'We won't encourage them anyway.'

'Mabel wants a whiskey.'

In the kitchen my grandmother poured the whiskey while I got the ice. She got an orange juice for Ron too, saying he'd had one the night before. When I got to the drawing room Mabel was on her own. She appeared to be dozing so I left the tray and got out of the room, fast.

My grandmother called to me from the front doorway as I stepped into the hall. 'Would you like to come for a walk?' she asked. 'Just to the cliff's edge. I go every day myself, winter and summer.'

She moved off and I followed her. She was no slouch. The path she used was the one I'd seen from my room earlier and the reality was much more overgrown than it had seemed from above. I had to skip and hop about to avoid nettles. My grandmother didn't seem to notice them, or the briars, and steamed along, talking as fast as she walked.

'There's an inlet at the end of the cliff where you can swim,' she said. 'I used to swim there for years myself. Not this summer though, not this summer. I told Ron about it but he wouldn't go without Mabel. Foolish man. She won't thank him. I've seen them before, the Rons and the Mabels. World's full of them, people living their lives through each other and never standing on their own two feet.' She stopped so suddenly that I bumped into her. She was frowning as she looked at me. 'You must always stand on your own two feet, Martha. Always.'

She started off again, at a slower pace this time but still nattering away. I followed only half listening. I didn't need to be told to stand on my own two feet; I had no intention of ever doing anything else.

The path petered out into a narrow track through furze. It ended at a grassy bank running around the cliff's edge, there to prevent people falling off. We stood and looked at the sea, vast and blue as ever. After a minute of this my grandmother pointed to a gap in the bank.

'That's the way down to the inlet,' she said.

I went along to have a look. At the other side of the gap there was a set of winding steps, with an iron rail along the side, which ran all the way down to a small, sandy beach. Even from the top I could see how clear and deep the water was, how gentle the waves. It would be a most wonderful, romantic and private place to go swimming with Manus.

'I suppose you can swim?' my grandmother asked. 'I don't want you drowning while you're here.'

'You don't have to worry.' I spoke absently, absorbed in my dream. I was still looking down, enjoying a particularly interesting private vision, when she turned and began to walk quickly back toward the house. When I caught up with her, I asked, by way of conversation, 'Did my mother ever swim there?'

She didn't break her stride but took a minute before answering. 'Indeed she did,' she said then. 'Your mother was a good swimmer when she was very young. I taught her myself. Lir House was a busy hotel in those days and guests with families used take her with them for whole days to that little beach. Things changed as she got older. She didn't care then for the company of guests.'

We were half way along the path when she slowed almost to a stop and began to wheeze, taking deep breaths. I didn't want to embarrass her by staring so I looked away, toward Lir House.

'How old is the hotel?' It was an idle question but, after a final deep breath, she answered enthusiastically. 'The original house was built a couple of hundred years ago and it's fifty-two years now since I began running it as a hotel. If walls could talk...' She stopped, looked at the house and gave a short, dark laugh, 'What a tale they'd tell. Your mother was born just as an Easter season got underway.'

'You mean she was actually born in the house?'

'Oh, yes, actually born in the house. Things were different in those days. I was able to direct things from my bed the next morning. She was a good baby. And she was a happy child. Now then...' She squared her shoulders and took a pocket-watch from somewhere in the folds of her skirt. 'Lorcan will be here soon to prepare dinner. Would you like to give him a hand? Or maybe you'd prefer to keep Ron and Mabel company?'

'I'll help with dinner.'

We finished the walk in silence and got to the house just as Chef O'Neill arrived in a spray of gravel.

'Oh, my stones! My poor, poor stones! Couldn't you please, walk the last fifty yards, Lorcan?' My grandmother shook her head wearily as he joined us by the door. She sounded half-hearted, though, as if she'd said the same thing many times before.

'Sorry Mrs Lambert.' Lorcan O'Neill's response, as

he pulled off his helmet, was automatic too. He ran a hand through curly hair and I was surprised at how long it was. And at his ponytail.

'Martha will help you with dinner,' my grandmother said. 'Ron and Mabel are still with us. What have you planned?'

'Chicken surprise.' He looked, very briefly, in my direction before disappearing into the darkness of the hallway.

Seconds later there came a string of low curses.

I hopped over the threshold ahead of my grandmother and, as my eyes adjusted, saw the chef on his knees. The helmet I'd left on the floor earlier was spinning crazily in front of him.

'That was a bloody stupid place to leave it.' He got to his feet and glared at me.

'I put it beside the wall.' I defended myself.

'Not close enough, you didn't.' He picked up the helmet, made a big thing of placing it against the wall and without a word went on down to the kitchen.

There was a small cough from the stairs and Ron, looking flustered and miserable, came down the last few steps.

'My wife is feeling peckish,' he said. 'We wondered when you might be serving dinner?'

'Won't be long now.' My grandmother's voice was cheerful. 'Should be on the table by seven o'clock.'

'But that's almost an hour away.' Ron's voice rose, then collapsed in a sort of despairing whimper. I began to inch towards the kitchen, away from his stricken face. You would think, to look at him, that my grandmother had announced the start of a nuclear war.

'The meal will be worth waiting for, I assure you.'

My grandmother was determinedly upbeat. 'We have an excellent iced soup to begin with and the chef tells me he's preparing a chicken special for the main course.'

I slipped through the kitchen door and escaped Ron's reply.

If he'd any sense he'd drive off to the nearest pub for the hour. Only he wouldn't do that, of course. Ron was absolute reject material.

'My grandmother says I'm to help you.' I stood beside Lorcan O'Neill in the kitchen. He was chopping onions and wearing a white apron that came nearly to the ground. Now that I looked at him properly he wasn't actually bad looking. I liked the combination of fair hair and dark eyes. The onions didn't seem to be affecting his tear ducts either.

'You can finish these.' He handed me a lethal looking knife.

The second I touched the onions my eyes began to water. I chopped away, my eyes streaming, sniffing loudly. The chef, busy doing something to a chicken, completely ignored me. I started to hum to myself as I worked. Since I don't have a note in my head this was calculated to annoy. The chef glowered at me. 'Those onions ready yet?' he demanded.

'Not yet.'

I beamed bravely through my tears and went on chopping, slowly. Muttering something I didn't catch he scooped up the onions I'd finished and threw them into a pan. The sound of their sizzling drowned my extra-loud sniffs as I picked up the last onion. He came back and stood over me as I sliced it, very carefully.

'Thanks a lot. You're a great help. Can you make a

salad?'

I dabbed my eyes with cold water and took a long minute before answering. 'Depends,' I said.

'Depends on what?'

'On the sort of salad you have in mind.'

'A green salad will do. There's oil and vingear on the table.' I'd never made a salad dressing before but I experimented with this and that. The result was approximately right and I felt pleased with myself.

The whole meal was ready just before seven. 'You can serve the soup now.' The chef put two bowls of his speciality on a tray. He sprinkled mint on top.

'Me? Serve?'

He looked at me coldly. 'Why not?'

'Well, I've never…'

'Always a first time. Do it from the right.'

He had a large knife in his hand as he held the door open for me. I lifted the tray, balanced it and took a deep breath.

'Hope your hands are clean,' he said as I passed him going out.

'Hope Mabel isn't sensitive to snotty-looking soup,' I said. It was feeble but was the best I could do in the circumstances.

Ron, Mabel and my grandmother were sitting around one end of the oval table when I arrived in the dining room. My grandmother immediately stood up.

'I won't keep you from your meal,' she said. 'I hope you enjoy it.' I was on my own. I tried not to look at Ron and Mabel as I put the tray down. I was aware of Mabel toying with a small handbell on the table and could feel her little eyes boring into me. I walked round the back of her chair and, from the right, placed the soup in front of her. I did the same for Ron. My ears rang in the silence.

'Everything all right?' I clutched the empty tray like a shield and prepared to leave.

'What is *this?*' Mabel found her voice at last. It was not a pretty sound.

'Iced apple soup,' I said. 'A chef's special.'

Mabel looked at me then. Really looked. If I'd told her it was a bowl of Ron's old socks, with seasoning, she couldn't have looked more venomous. I half expected her to hiss and moved back from the table, just in case.

'It looks like…' Mabel paused. 'It's disgusting. I want some proper soup. Tomato. Or oxtail.'

'Why don't you try it first, dear?' Ron interrupted her with another of his little coughs. He dipped his own spoon into the soup, tasted delicately. 'Mmm. It's very good really. Just the thing in this hot weather.'

'Afraid we've got no tomato,' I said. 'No oxtail either.'

'What sort of hotel *is* this?' Mabel demanded. But she picked up her spoon. I backed away as the soup began to disappear into her fat face. I didn't quite make it. Before I could turn tail for the kitchen she fixed me with a basilisk stare.

'I hope the main course is more substantial,' she snapped.

'My wife likes her food.' Ron's squeak was unnecessary. Anyone could see Mabel *lived* for her food.

'What sort of chicken dish are we getting?' Mabel was on her third bread roll.

'It has onions in it.'

35

'Onions!' Mabel echoed my descriptive efforts with something like a snarl. 'I'm not at all partial to fowl. I sincerely hope we are to be served this chicken with something more than onions.'

'There's salad. A green salad.'

I was saved from further explaining by my grandmother. She swept into the room with a sheet of paper in her hand.

'The wine list,' she announced. 'Sorry to have kept you waiting.'

I bolted for the door and into the kitchen.

'I'm not going back in there.' I threw myself into a chair and the tray on to the table. 'That woman deserves to starve. She's a grade-A cow.'

'She's a guest,' Lorcan O'Neill said pompously. He was ladling the chicken on to two plates. It looked and smelled all right.

'*You* serve her then,' I said. 'I've done my waiting stint for tonight. You've no idea what she's like.'

'I don't *care* what she's like. And you're not even half waythrough your stint.' He said this in a matter-of-fact voice and, while I gaped in disbelief, put the plates on the tray and covered them with silver warmers. 'There's dessert and coffee and the wash-up still to go.'

'You must be joking.' I sat up straight and gawked at him. I couldn't believe my ears. 'I'm not taking orders from you. And I'm certainly not doing the wash-up. That's your job.'

He didn't answer, just put a dish of vegetables on the tray and covered it too. He added the salad and shoved the lot across the table at me.

'Why don't you stop being a pain in the ass and get

in there with the food. It'll go cold.'

'You can go stuff yourself!' I stood up and pushed the tray back at him. 'And you can serve your own food. I'm not going back to take abuse about your cooking from that woman.'

'It's all right, Martha my dear, I'll do it.' My grandmother's voice made us both jump. She was standing just inside the door and I wondered how much of our row she'd heard. 'I quite agree with you,' she went on, 'Mabel isn't at all pleasant. But she'll have to be fed all the same.'

She smiled as she put the wine list on the table and spoke to Lorcan. 'They'd like a bottle of house white,' she said to him and then, to me, 'Maybe you could bring up the wine, Martha, while I do the food?'

She lifted the tray and without waiting for an answer turned for the door. The way she balanced it I just knew the tray was too heavy for her. Annoyed and embarrassed I started after her.

'Leave it,' Lorcan O'Neill's voice menaced in my ear. 'Just bring the wine.'

He got a bottle from the fridge, took the cork out and wrapped a white napkin around it. I wanted to say something incredibly cutting but couldn't think of a thing. I reached for the wine but he held on to it and looked me nastily and self-righteously in the eye.

'Your grandmother's a decent woman,' he said. 'I don't know anything about your family situation or how she's got herself stuck with a silly cow like you for the summer. But you're here and while I'm running this kitchen I expect you to make yourself useful.' He handed me the wine. 'Your grandmother can do with the help anyway so you can stop acting the spoilt bitch.'

'Look, you.' I was in a cold fury, shaking at the injustice of it all. 'I didn't ask to come here. I'm here because my grandmother asked for me and I was *sent*. I don't want to be here. This…this…backwoods tip is not my idea of a place to spend a summer.'

'Tough'. He shrugged and turned away. If I'd had anything liquid handy I'd have thrown it over him. Without turning round he said, 'The wine's getting warm.'

In the dining room my grandmother chatted away as she served, impervious to her guests' silence.

'We use free-range birds. They're from a local farm so I can vouch for them myself. The vegetables are grown locally too. There now.' She stepped back. 'I'll leave you to enjoy your meal. And I see that Martha's brought the wine.'

She smiled at me as I poured, Ron first so that he could taste—I'm not a complete philistine. When he nodded, after a nervous look at Mabel, I filled his glass. Mabel, who was eating very fast, didn't even look up as I filled hers. I put the bottle on the table and left them to it.

My grandmother was waiting for me again in the hallway. She took my arm and led me away from the door.

'Well.' She gave a low, throaty chuckle. 'You've had a baptism of fire and no mistake! There's a Mabel for every season and you've handled this summer's model very well. Now, about Lorcan.' She lowered her voice. I wanted to tell her to stop but didn't think there would be much point. 'He's very earnest about his job, which is a good thing. But if you take him with a grain of salt you'll get along much better.' She laughed at her little joke and I smiled politely. Then she became serious. 'Poor lad's grown old before his time. His father ran off a couple of years ago so he's has had to do a lot of the fathering in the family. He's a good lad. But you just do what you feel able to around here and that'll be fine. I don't want you grumbling. I hate grumblers. Never complained myself.'

I could believe this. It was hard to imagine her sitting down for a moan. The picture she painted of Lorcan O'Neill, on the other hand, was just too good to be true.

We had reached the kitchen door when the handbell rang loudly in the dining room. My grandmother rolled her eyes. 'Second helpings for Mabel by the sound of it,' she said.

'I'll sort her out,' I said quickly, my voice sounding to me only vaguely like my own. I don't usually use a firm, decisive tone, mainly because I'm not usually either of those things. But it seemed important just then to prove to myself that I could deal with Mabel.

Mabel saw me crossing the dining room but didn't stop ringing the handbell until I reached the table.

'We'll have more chicken,' she said, 'and more vegetables too.'

'Of course.' I put on a firm, polite voice and looked right at her as I picked up the empty vegetable dishes. What I saw, and couldn't stop staring at, was the sauce she'd dribbled on to the pink of her vast smock.

'Thank you,' Ron pulled his doleful face into a sort of smile as I turned to go. Mabel said nothing. Neither of them said a word when I returned with the food.

In the kitchen my grandmother had laid three places

at the table. I wasn't hungry but I sat and nibbled anyway. My grandmother ate with relish. 'Very good, Lorcan,' she said when she'd finished.

'Thanks, Mrs Lambert,' he said with a smile, looking quite human and jerked his head in the direction of the dining room. 'Will they be here for dinner tomorrow night too?'

'They haven't quite decided.' My grandmother looked first at Lorcan, then at me. 'But I've made a decision myself. I've decided that this glorious summer we're having deserves to be enjoyed. We shouldn't have to spend it humouring any more Rons and Mabels. I've got only two firm bookings for the rest of the summer and when they arrive I will take them in. But I intend refusing all others. Unless they be European royalty or Irish rock stars of course.' She laughed and shook her head. 'It's too late anyway to impress my bank manager with a busy season. So when Ron and Mabel depart we'll relax.'

She sat back and looked at us. I smiled, nervously. The prospect of rattling around an empty Lir House filled me with misgivings. Lorcan O'Neill smiled too, even more nervously. *He* was probably worried about his job.

'Better take down the sign so, Mrs. Lambert,' he said, 'or you'll have people driving up here and upsetting your gravel for nothing...'

'You're quite right, Lorcan. Maybe you'd take it down for me on the way home? Then you can bring it back up with you tomorrow night. I'd like you to continue looking after the kitchen for me, if you would. Even when it's only Martha and myself we'll enjoy being cooked for. Won't we, Martha?'

I muttered something vaguely agreeable and studied the grain of the table. I thought she was being far too nice to him.

'Great! I'll work out a set of—' His voice was full of gratitude. He didn't even try to hide it. The handbell, ringing again in the dining room, cut short his grovelling.

'I'll deal with it this time.' My grandmother was imperious. 'Cut me a couple of portions of your cheesecake, Lorcan. I'll take it to them for dessert.'

He cut two enormous portions and she went off to the dining room with them.

It felt really awkward, being left alone in the kitchen with Lorcan O'Neill. He began to clear up and, for a while, I moseyed around, looking in cupboards. After a bit though, and with a huge sigh to show what a bore I thought it all was, I began to help. We worked in complete silence and had almost finished by the time my grandmother came back.

'Ron and Mabel will be going in the morning,' she announced. 'I'll take them some coffee and continue our chat. They've developed a keen interest in the coastline south of here.'

This time, as soon as she left, Lorcan O'Neill whipped off his apron.

'See you tomorrow,' he said curtly. His T-shirt had a slogan on the front that said, 'I'm not only perfect, I can cook too.' I raised an eyebrow. He pretended not to notice, picked up his helmet and went.

Once I was completely alone I realised how tired I was. A lot had happened in one day. I thought about joining my grandmother and the others in the dining room and then thought again. Even an early night had more to recommend it. But first I would phone my mother, forestall any complaints.

Pushing open the dining room door I heard Mabel give a squeaky laugh. My grandmother was pointing to something on a map and Ron was dozing. When I asked about the phone my grandmother said, 'Of course' but said nothing about talking to my mother herself.

When my mother answered, she lectured about not calling earlier and reminded me how expensive long-distance calls were. I was really sorry I'd bothered.

The red helmet was still in the hallway. Passing, I gave it the gentlest of kicks and landed it back exactly where it had been earlier. With any luck Mr Self-righteous O'Neill would trip over it again.

In bed I tried to read but fell asleep after a few pages. I dreamt of Manus, wonderful dreams in which he held me tight, told me his life was empty without me and promised to follow me to the ends of the earth.

CHAPTER FIVE

Ron and Mabel left early the next morning. My grandmother and I watched from the door as he piled their bags into the back of the car, did a wide turn and careered uncertainly down the avenue. He drove with squealing brakes all the way to the main road.

My grandmother snorted. 'That man'll have a coronary within two years,' she predicted.

I left her muttering away to herself and went for a walk around the outside of the house. The walls were crumbly and full of cracks. I sat for a while, leaning against the front, and trying to imagine what the overgrown garden might have looked like once. It was another sunny day and at my back the wall of the house was already heating up. I decided to go for a swim.

'Would you like to come to the village with me afterwards?' my grandmother asked when I told her my intention. 'I go once a week. Dave Furlong takes me in his taxi. He'll be calling at midday.'

I said OK and wandered off to the cove. The water was delicious, the sand warm and the solitude deeply depressing. By the time midday and the taxi arrived, the trip to the village had assumed the proportions of a mega-adventure.

Not that Dave Furlong contributed much by way of excitement. He was taciturn, to say the least of it. His taxi was an old and well polished Ford Sierra filled with No Smoking signs, air fresheners and holy medals. When I opened the window to breathe he said, 'Close it!' so loudly that I jumped in my seat.

'Better humour him or he'll leave us to walk home.' My grandmother's whisper was so deep he couldn't not have heard her.

'Can't you use someone else?' I didn't even try to whisper myself. She shook her head.

'He's the only one around,' she said, patting me on the hand. She looked out of the window for the rest of the journey and I had a good look at what she was wearing. She wore a black straw hat, high and precarious looking since her hair was piled into it. She had a black-beaded cardigan and under it a long grey dress. Around her neck she had tied two scarves. Altogether she looked like a scarecrow.

Faylinn just about qualified as a village. Its single street straggled around a church and large, new-looking building with Community Centre written across it. We entered the village by driving around a small, circular green with a Celtic cross in the middle. Once on the street we drove slowly past a post office with shoes and T-shirts in the window, a butcher, newsagent and two pubs. We stopped at last outside a supermarket and my grandmother looked at her watch.

'Give us an hour and a half, Dave,' she said.

Dave didn't reply and we got out.

A bell jingled as we went into the supermarket and Lorcan O'Neill looked up from something he was reading by the cash register. There was a single, central aisle lined with bread, fruit, vegetables and breakfast cereals. Everything else was on shelves around the walls. Some of these were so high that a wooden step-ladder stood by for customer use. I wondered if any of them ever fell off.

'You're late today, Mrs Lambert.' Lorcan O'Neill spoke as if I weren't there.

'I am,' she agreed and looked at two large boxes on the counter. 'And I see you've got my order packed up. I want to add a few things.' She picked up a tomato and felt it. 'Are these the best you have?'

'No. They're Dutch. I've got Irish ones in the back.'

He got up and went through a door. It stayed open behind him and immediately the wails of a small child filled the shop.

'Say hello to your mother for me,' my grandmother called. The wails stopped, briefly, then began again, only much louder. Lorcan O'Neill returned with a box of tomatoes. He looked hassled.

'She says to return the compliment. She'd be out to see you only she's a bit tied up at the moment.'

He dumped the tomatoes and went back to close the door. Before he got to it there was a crash and a second older-sounding child began to yell along with the first.

Lorcan O'Neill disappeared through the door again and came back about a minute later with a small, stubborn-looking kid of about five.

'Sit there and don't even *breathe* until your lunch is ready.' He plonked the small boy on top of a crate and came back to help my grandmother to pick out tomatoes.

'Sorry about the delay,' he said.

'I'm in no hurry,' my grandmother replied easily. 'How are you today, Kevin?' She called to the small boy who, by way of answer, kicked the crate with one of his swinging legs. Lorcan O'Neill weighed the tomatoes and put them in a bag.

'Will you be going into Wexford before the end of the week?' my grandmother asked him.

'Should be going in on Saturday afternoon.'

'Good. You might pick up a few things for me. Martha will go along to help you.' She turned to me. 'You'll enjoy Wexford,' she said.

I thought that this might well be true but didn't fancy the idea of going with Mr Jack-of-all-Trades O'Neill. I said nothing that would commit me to going and hung around, looking through the shelves, while my grandmother finished her shopping. We left everything there and we went along the street to the butcher, then on to the newsagent. The excitement of it all was really getting to me when my grandmother suggested the pub.

'A nice cold Guinness is what I need,' she said and that was exactly what the barman, unasked, put in front of her as soon as we sat down.

'I'll have a rock shandy,' I said.

'Pint or glass?'

'Pint. Please.'

He went away and I looked around. It was a dark, comfortable pub and, even at that time of day, had a good sprinkling of customers. Most of them nodded and called greetings to my grandmother. The barman came back with my rock shandy and stood as I took a gulp.

'This the granddaughter?' he asked my grandmother. You would have thought, the way he asked it, that I was deaf, blind and stupid.

'Yes, Tom. This is Martha.' My grandmother put down her own drink. 'Martha, this is Tom Brady. He was a friend of your mother's a long time ago.'

I looked at him. He was almost bald and looked a lot older than my mother. He smiled at me. 'Is your mother keeping well?' he asked.

'She's fine,' I said.

'Will she be coming down herself to see us this summer?'

'I don't think so. I don't know.'

'It's a while now since she visited. But she's busy, I suppose, like the rest of us. Still, now that you're here she might find the time to come down. You don't look a bit like her. You've more the look of your grandmother about you.'

Someone called to him and he went back to the bar. I watched as he laughed loudly at something that was said. 'Was he a good friend of my mother's?' I asked.

'He used to walk her up the road from school when they were both very young,' my grandmother said with a smile. 'He was a kind boy. And thoughtful. He hasn't changed.' She drained her glass. 'Time to go,' she said.

At the counter the barman refused to take any money from her. 'Times are not so hard that we can't offer a granddaughter of yours a drink,' he said and winked at me. 'Enjoy yourself now.'

'I will,' I said, with heavy irony. He didn't seem to notice.

Later, while I was helping my grandmother to unpack the groceries in the kitchen at Lir House, I asked her something that had been on my mind since the pub.

'Have you never minded living here on your own, grandmother?'

She didn't answer straight away and I thought she'd gone all huffy. But when she turned from the fridge the frown on her face was more puzzled than annoyed.

'Why no, Martha, not at all. I liked it. I wouldn't have had it any other way. And of course, I wasn't alone at all really. I had my guests.' She laughed. 'They were often more company than I wanted. And of course I've had this fellow living with me for eight or nine years now, haven't I, Fiachra?'

She scooped up the wretched cat who, smelling the food no doubt, had come skulking into the kitchen.

'But what about when you wanted someone to talk to? You know, share things with.'

'Never felt the need. Never thought I should share my life with someone just because people thought I should. Life's an insecure business Martha, but it's important to maintain independence. Don't you agree?'

'Yes.' I hadn't thought a great deal about it but as I listened I found myself agreeing, more or less, with everything she said. She put the cat down and began putting food into his dish.

'Make your life your own, Martha, that's all I'm saying.' She looked at me with a wrinkly grin. 'Do it this very minute. Go on, find yourself something to do.'

She made shooing noises and waved her hands. I went. It was obvious she wanted to be on her own. I went to my room and wrote to Naomi. I wrote about the village and about Ron and Mabel and made them all sound stupidly funny, which was easy to do. I told her about the cove too, and the good swimming there. I finished off by telling her to write to me with news of

Manus. But even as I did this I hoped desperately that he would have phoned himself by the time she replied to me.

To stave off a fit of loneliness, brought on by writing the letter, I got my camera and went outside to look for some shots.

Nothing about the sea and cliffs turned me on but when I faced back to Lir House I got an interesting shot of my grandmother watching me from a window. She was standing very still, the way she'd stood when I first saw her. The sun, shining on the glass, blanked out her face. It was a spooky, interesting shot.

I was making myself a sandwich when Lorcan O'Neill arrived to prepare dinner. Fiachra came into the kitchen with him.

'How're the yelling kids?' I asked.

'Still yelling.' He gave a tight grin and wrapped himself in the apron.

'They your small brothers or what?'

'Right first time—they're my brothers. I've a sister too but she's in London for the summer. The boys are all right most of the time; they're just having a bad day today. Have you got any brothers, or what, at home?'

'One brother. Garrett. He's all right too, when he's not being a bore about figures and economics and things.'

We were having a conversation! And it might have gone a lot further too if Fiachra hadn't jumped on table just then. He probably did it on purpose.

'Get out of here, you scavenger!' Lorcan leaped at him. 'Go on, out! You'll get fed later.' Fiachra, sullen and poisonous looking, jumped down and vanished through the door. 'He smells the plaice. I got some for dinner. Hope you like fish.'

I said I did and he became super-busy with sauces and breadcrumbs.

I wanted to ask him what people in the village thought of my grandmother but commonsense told me this was not the moment. It wasn't the night either because, straight away after we'd eaten, he zoomed off.

A German guest, one of my grandmother's 'firm bookings', arrived on a bicycle early next morning. He was tall, skinny and a vegetarian. His eating habits didn't faze the Lir House cook however and that evening we had nut loaf for dinner. I gave a hand myself with the making of it.

The new guest's name was Otto. He'd been to Lir House before and seemed glad to be making a return visit. He was gentle, very polite and quite old to be cycling around for his holidays. He was at least forty. He liked to spend his time outdoors, he said, just cycling and looking.

I'd woken that morning with a be-nice-to-Lorcan resolution forming in my head. It was, I knew, my survival instinct at work. He was the only person my own age around and, unlike my grandmother, I liked to have people to talk to. I was prepared to forgive and forget his righteous lecture of the first night, providing he abandoned his posing superiority. I was going to give him a chance to do that anyway.

'So what're you going to give our vegetarian guest?' I was full of cheer as I bounced into the kitchen.

'Nut loaf. Salad. You'll be getting the same. If you don't like the sound of it you'd better rustle up something else for yourself.'

'Nut loaf sounds great,' I said, ignoring the fact that

he wasn't prepared to cook separately for me. 'Do you want me to do anything?'

'Not yet.'

I watched silently, with what I hoped was an intelligent expression, as he laid out breadcrumbs, tomatoes, nuts and an array of seasonings. He was wearing jeans and a black T-shirt. No apron. I noticed for the first time that he had an earring in one ear, quite a flash job too. Under different circumstances, if he wasn't such a prat and if he wasn't so self-important, I *might* have fancied him.

There were too many ifs, unfortunately. And of course there was Manus.

He caught me looking and lobbed a green pepper my way. 'Chop that,' he said, 'and melt some butter in a pan. I'll do the onions.' He grinned and it all became quite friendly. We got the nut loaf together in record time. While it was cooking he handed me a corkscrew.

'Open a bottle of red wine, will you? Nothing vintage, I want it for a sauce.' He indicated a door at the other end of the kitchen and, obediently I scampered in that direction. Behind the door there was a deep, chilly, stone-walled pantry. The big surprise was that, from floor to ceiling, it was filled with bottles of wine. I stepped inside.

'There's quite a cellar here! Is this for the guests we don't have or is my old gran a secret tippler?'

'It's hotel stock.'

My search for a cheapo bottle of red wasn't easy. I don't know much about wine but *Grand Crus* are not plonk and there were an awful lot of those on the racks. I eventually found something that I thought was moderate.

'Will this do?'

The chef looked briefly at the label and nodded. 'Still hopping mad about being sent here?' he asked.

I wrinkled my nose, rolled my eyes a bit. 'Yup. But I'm not mad at my grandmother any more. She seems OK. So far.'

'How come you never came to stay with her before?'

'I'm not sure why. Really. You know what families are like.' It would have been too complicated to tell him my mother and grandmother had a big feud going. Especially when I didn't know myself what it was all about.

He had enough cop-on not to press things further. I warmed to him, feeling as I got to know him better that he was not so self-righteous after all. As we waited for the nut loaf to finish cooking I asked, 'What do you do for a good time around here?'

'Depends.'

'Depends on what?'

'On who you're with. On what you feel like doing.'

'What do people feel like doing on Saturday nights?'

'That depends too. On the same things.'

'What about Saturday afternoon?' I asked. 'Can I come with you to Wexford?'

'Why not? I'll pick you up around two.' He opened the oven door. 'We're ready for lift-off.'

Later than night, with Otto reading in one armchair and my grandmother asleep in another, I phoned Manus. I did it on impulse. Looking at Otto and my grandmother had filled me with a mad desire to share the excitement of a Lir House evening with him.

His mother answered, sounding surprised to hear

me. Manus's mother is very glamorous. She is also very vague.

'He's not at home, dear,' she said. She calls everyone dear, except Manus. She calls him darling. All the time. He doesn't seem to notice. 'It's a bit early for him to be in. Do you want to leave a message?'

'Oh, it's not important. Could you just tell him I rang? Martha that is.' She's the sort of woman you have to remind of things. 'I'll give you my number too. He might want to get in touch with me.' I'd already given Manus the number but he was always losing things.

'If you like, dear.' Mrs. Byrne didn't sound encouraging but I gave her the number anyway and rang off.

I went upstairs, lay on my mother's bed and thought of Manus. The phone call had brought home to me, all over again, the reality of our separating. He was only a hundred miles away but he might as well have been at the other end of the world. I had no way of knowing how he was, what he was feeling.

Even if he ever thought of me.

I undressed and slipped into bed. The night was hot and the sheet clung to me. I fell asleep wondering how I should handle things when Manus came to Lir House.

CHAPTER SIX

The next morning's big event was a visit from the postman. He was in the doorway, talking to my grandmother, as I came down the stairs. They made a great silhouette. The postman was small and round and my grandmother, who was wearing a shawl, loomed over him like a large crow. As I turned to go back for my camera they moved into the hall and the picture was gone.

'Good morning to you.' The postman gave me a little wave and I went on down to join them. Close up, his face was red and his eyes tiny and inquisitive. He winked at me, beaming widely. 'It's a great morning to be alive,' he said.

'I suppose it is.' I stood close to my grandmother.

'This is my granddaughter, Martha. She'll be spending the summer here.'

The postman cut short my grandmother's introduction. 'Flynn's the name, Con Flynn,' he said. I took his proffered hand, carefully, and he pumped mine up and down. 'You're the image of your grandmother, God bless you. And how're you enjoying this part ofthe country?'

'I haven't seen much of it yet.' I took my hand back.

'You'll be a great help to your grandmother for the summer. Pity you weren't able to come before, in the days when the hotel was busier. But better late than never, isn't that right, Mrs Lambert?'

'That's right, Con.' My grandmother's tone was dry.

'Do you have anything for me?'

'Ah, yes.' Shaking his head, as if he'd just remembered why he was there, the postman handed over a letter. My grandmother looked at it briefly and slipped it into a pocket.

'French stamp on that letter,' the postman said. 'I suppose that means you've visitors coming from France?'

'I'll know when I've had time to read it.'

My grandmother smiled, taking the edge off the words. I'd have told him to mind his own business if it had been me. Otto came down the stairs just then and the postman called a loud 'Good Morning' to him too as he crossed the hall. He looked a bit startled and dived for the cover of the dining room without answering.

'I'll get Otto's breakfast.' I made the offer partly to get away and partly to show the postman that I was capable of helping around the place.

'Be sure you give him a good feed of porridge,' the postman laughed. 'Those fellows on bicycles need plenty of nourishment. Well, I'll be off now.' He looked hopefully at my grandmother. 'You're not going to open the letter then?'

'All in good time, Con.' She was curt. 'All in good time.'

The postman sighed and his bright little eyes fixed themselves on mine. 'You'll be all right if you make as fine a woman as your grandmother, Martha,' he said. 'But please God you won't suffer the same misfortune in life.'

'We won't delay you any longer, Con.' There was no mistaking the sliver of ice in my grandmother's voice.

'Drive carefully now, and good day to you.'

The postman, with a wide wave, moved off at last.

'What did he mean by your "misfortune"?' I asked as he turned his green van. My grandmother gave an exasperated sigh.

'Don't pay any attention to that man,' she said. 'The drive up here makes him nervous and the drive down terrifies him. The whole thing makes him talk a lot of nonsense. Now, I must check with Otto about his plans for the day.'

I knew she was avoiding my question. But since I couldn't very well force her to answer I went off to the kitchen and made Otto's breakfast. He was a yoghurt and apple person so there wasn't much to do. I'd finished laying a tray for him, complete with herb tea, when my grandmother joined me.

'Otto's going for a long cycle today,' she said. 'So I'll need to make him a packed lunch.'

She sat at the table, looking very tired. I hadn't noticed her looking tired before and wondered if, like my mother, she had problems sleeping. My mother becomes agitated when she talks about her insomnia so I avoided asking my grandmother about her sleeping habits. I picked up the tray.

'Kettle's boiled if you want tea or coffee,' I said. She didn't seem to hear me. She had taken the letter out of her pocket and was looking at it.

Otto, with maps spread across the table, was in chatty mood.

He asked me all sorts of intelligent questions about the countryside around, very few of which I was able to answer.

When I got back to the kitchen my grandmother was sitting very still, reading the letter.

'Bad news?'

'Mmm,' was all she said so I boiled up the kettle again and made coffee. I put a cup in front of her and sat opposite. She had folded the letter back into its envelope by then and was drumming her fingers gently on the table.

'Good news, I think.' She took a sip of the coffee. 'My other booking has written to say he will be arriving a week earlier than planned and will stay longer too. He's a return guest, like Otto, and knows what to expect here. I'm sure you and I can look after him together, for as long as he wants to stay.'

'What's he like?'

I was hoping she'd say he was younger than Otto, charming and dark-eyed, but commonsense prevailed. Why would someone like that want to holiday in the deadly boring Irish countryside?

'It's been a good while since he last visited.' Her answer immediately ruled out youth. 'So I can't tell you what he's like now. He could be very amusing, as I remember.'

'What's he called and what part of France does he come from?'

'He's from Bordeaux and his name is Maurice Dupont. Maybe you can learn some French from him. It's a very useful language.'

The prospect of French irregular verbs almost brought on a fever. 'Haven't seen Fiachra this morning.' I didn't want to see him either but it seemed a safe change of subject.

'I fed him earlier. He's gone off about his business.' My grandmother drummed the table again. 'I think, Martha, that we will give the house and grounds a bit of a freshening up. It's as well to have the place looking its best for the autumn. I'll probably have to sell then, you know. I'll get the grounds cut back so as we can enjoy the walks and I'll ask Joan Walsh up from the village to help us spruce up the house. I think it's best to do it before Monsieur Dupont gets here.'

That was Thursday. Maurice Dupont was due to arrive the following Tuesday. The five days in between were some of the most active in my entire life.

Joan Walsh from the village was a thin, busy woman and it was obvious she'd worked in Lir House before. She drew up a battle plan for the big clean-up, with herself as a hands-on commander. First the curtains were taken from the windows and sent to the cleaners by taxi. Then the entire place was scrubbed clean—floors, ceilings, walls, cupboards, furniture even. Rugs were taken out and beaten to within an inch of their pile and baths and toilets were treated to enough chemicals to kill a plague of locusts.

Fiachra disappeared after the first day's activity. Just took himself off. My grandmother was philosophical. 'He'll be back,' she said. 'He hates discomfort so he's gone to find himself pleasanter lodgings for a few days. He'll find them too,' she laughed. 'Tom cats are like that.'

Poor old Otto wasn't so lucky. He came and went in a daze through all the activity. My grandmother was really nice to him in the evenings and saw to it that he always got exactly what he wanted for dinner. He seemed quite sad to be leaving when he cycled off for the last time on Sunday.

While the house shed its dust and grime the rhododenderons and smaller trees around the house lost their branches. A man called Liam hacked away at them, every day from morning till night. He refused to come inside but every hour, on the hour, my grandmother sent me out to him with a cup of tea and a cheese sandwich. I tried to talk to him but got nowhere. He was your original silent, backwoods type.

And he knew what he was doing. By Sunday the gardens had become quite civilised. On Monday morning he arrived with an almighty lawn-mower and by that evening the cliff-top looked almost suburban.

I worked hard myself, especially after Saturday. That was the day I realised what a fool I'd been with my be-nice-to-Lorcan-O'Neill resolution. The sheer physical labour helped me get over my anger at my own stupidity.

On Friday, when he'd made arrangements to call for me on Saturday for the trip to Wexford, I'd actually begun to think that Lorcan O'Neill was OK. 'I'll be meeting a few mates,' he said. 'You can come along or wander off on your own, whatever you like.'

'I'll come along,' I said. 'But I'd like to find a camera shop.'

'No problem. We'll do that first. I'll call for you about one o'clock.'

When he hadn't arrived by 1.30 on Saturday I started to worry. Maybe he'd fallen off the bike. Joan passed me several times, sniffing loudly, as I sat on the stairs waiting. She hadn't approved of me taking the afternoon off.

I went outside to get away from her silent reproach but Liam was working with an electric saw and the noise was even more annoying than Joan's sniffing.

By half past two, when I picked up the ringing phone, I knew Lorcan O'Neill wasn't coming.

'Martha, I'm sorry.'

It was an hour and a half too late to be sorry and I

told him so. 'Look, there was a problem. There was nothing I could do about it.'

'You could have got in touch earlier.'

'I wasn't anywhere near a phone.'

'Maybe you should learn to send smoke signals, if phones are so rare in this part of the country.' I saw no reason to be nice to him.

'Oh, come on, Martha. I didn't do it deliberately. I'll explain when I come up this evening.

'Don't bother. It really doesn't matter.'

I hung up, stormed off to the kitchen, grabbed a handful of cleaning things and prepared to get back to work. But even as I raged about Lorcan O'Neill I knew that he was only partly the cause of my fury. The fact that Manus had not yet been in touch was really beginning to get to me.

I went to Joan to see what she wanted me to do. With a grunt that sounded very like satisfaction she set me to cleaning the windows.

Not since the day they were put into the house had they been cleaned so well. I worked until sweat dripped from my forehead and upper lip. When my T-shirt stuck to me I prised it loose, fanned myself and went on working.

I got a lot of things out of my system that afternoon. Temporarily anyway. By the time Lorcan O'Neill arrived at five o'clock I had covered a great deal of glass. But I kept at it, pretending not to notice when he hovered at the end of the ladder on which I was perched. He knew I could see him in the beautifully shining window and, after a minute, shrugged and went away.

Dad rang while my grandmother and I were eating dinner. At least my grandmother was eating. I'd decided I couldn't stomach another O'Neill vegetarian special. I felt almost weepy when I heard him on the phone. Even if he *is* peace-loving to the point of feebleness I do like my Dad.

'The house is very quiet without you,' he said. I could just see him, squinting through his heavy specs at the silent, dust-free hallway that would never, ever need a major clean-up.

'Well, that's what you all wanted, isn't it?' I still wasn't ready to forgive him for the way he'd allowed my mother pack me off.

'True. That's what we wanted. But we still miss you. All of us.'

This shocked me into momentary silence. I knew he meant it, for himself anyway.

'How's your grandmother?' he asked, before I could think of anything to say.

'She's fine. We're doing a big clean-up here.'

We chatted for a few minutes more and then Garrett came on the line. He and I had a bit of a laugh, something we hadn't had for a long time. Maybe my being away was doing *some* good. My mother came on the line last of all and we were quite civil to one another for about a minute. She didn't ask to speak to her mother.

By Monday afternoon, when Joan took her wages and jumped on her bike to go home, Lir House smelled richly of polish and disinfectant. It looked good too, cared for and brighter. My grandmother and I sat in the drawing room after she left. I'd noticed her flagging several times during the day but, even when Joan told her to, she hadn't rested. She looked pretty exhausted now, sunk in a chair with her eyes closed.

'I'm glad that's over.' She opened her eyes and

looked around. 'Poor old house. It deserves to look its best more often. And now, Martha, you and I deserve a treat. What would you say to a glass of good wine?'

I said yes, naturally, and she told me what to get. We had a glass each and relaxed in the polish-smelling peace. It seemed like a good time to get personal.

'Have you ever left Lir House, Grandmother?' I asked.

'Left it? What do you mean, Martha?'

'Well, lived anywhere else, for instance.'

'No. Never.' She became thoughtful. 'I have lived for this house. Some would say it's a mistake, living for a house. But I found it a most satisfactory way to spend my life. A house is a much more durable prospect than a person, you know. As long as you care for it, it will stand by you. There are no such guarantees with a person.' She paused, looked around the room and wrinkled her nose. 'That polish! Open the window a bit wider, Martha, will you please?'

I did as she asked, my mind buzzing with the question I wanted to ask her. Was she telling me that my grandfather had left her before he died? Or was it just her way of saying that by dying he'd left her? I didn't get a chance to find out, not then anyway.

Lorcan O'Neill ruined the moment by arriving, noisily, just as I raised the window. My grandmother, with obvious effort, pulled herself out of the armchair. 'My poor gravel,' she sighed. 'I must talk to Lorcan about menus. We must plan for Monsieur Dupont's stay.'

CHAPTER SEVEN

Maurice Dupont arrived in a taxi. I was coming back from a swim, across the newly cut lawn. As it drew to the front of the house I broke into a trot.

He was old and he used a stick. Those were the first things I noticed as he got out of the taxi. He was small and not particularly worldly looking either. Disappointed, I stopped dead in my tracks.

As I stood there, disappointment turning to resignation, my grandmother came out the front door. She was dressed in her black-and-white outfit, ready to do her welcoming bit. The taxi-driver piled luggage beside her on the portico, took money from Maurice Dupont and drove off. My grandmother raised a hand in greeting and her guest moved forward, limping a little, to take it. They shook hands formally and my grandmother led the way slowly into the house.

Filled with a feeling of anti-climax I went up to my room. I lay on the bed, fully intending to get up again in a few minutes, but somehow fell asleep. I slept for nearly an hour and washed my hair when I woke up. I was sitting in the window, letting it dry in the sun, when my grandmother called me. She was waiting in the hallway when I got downstairs.

'I'd like you to meet our guest before Lorcan gets here,' she said and led me into the drawing room.

Maurice Dupont stood and bowed deeply when she introduced us. 'I am delighted to make your acquaintance, *Mademoiselle*.' His French accent was strong but he didn't try to kiss my hand, which was just as well. I'd have been mortified. He had nice brown eyes and a friendly smile but he was almost bald.

'*Enchantée, Monsieur*,' I stuttered a bit, uncertain. He laughed and leant forward on his cane. It had a silver top and ferrule.

'I intend to speak only English while I am here,' he said. 'So you will not be obliged to practice your French on me.'

'That's good news.' I grinned with relief. 'I've a bit of a problem with French.'

'She is not an easy language,' he conceded and waved his cane in the direction of the window. 'But maybe we can share something else? I like to paint watercolours and your *grandmère* tells me you are a photographer. Maybe we can work together, sometimes?'

The suggestion didn't exactly grab me by the throat. I like to be alone when I'm taking pictures. Something of this must have shown in my face because Maurice Dupont, with a small laugh, immediately said, 'But only, *chère mademoiselle*, if you have time and would find it interesting.'

We had been standing all this time and I realised he was waiting for me to sit down. I dropped into the nearest armchair, which was beside my grandmother. He sat back into his; then leaned forward on his cane, smiling and nodding at both of us. I thought him quite comical, but nice.

'You have been to France?' he asked.

Before I could admit to this gap in my travel experience Fiachra came prowling through the open window. He'd come back the night before and had carried on with a great deal of miaowing through the newly cleaned rooms. He started it again now, circling Maurice Dupont with his back arched. I'd never seen him so unfriendly, which was saying something. My grandmother called to him and he jumped onto her lap. He lay there, his tail slowly swishing as he looked murderously at the new guest.

'Behave, Fiachra.' My grandmother was stern but the cat's tail swished if anything with greater intent.

'He is not happy to see me,' said Maurice Dupont, 'and I do not think he will change his mind.' He held out a friendly hand to Fiachra and got a snarling hiss for his trouble. He sighed, a deeply French sigh, and spread his hands. 'He is a loyal animal,' he said.

'In his way,' my grandmother agreed. She stroked Fiachra and he began to purr complacently. Maurice Dupont studied him carefully.

'He has a name?' he asked, and when my grandmother told him, tried valiantly to pronounce it. He gave up with a shrug and a mock glare at the cat.

Maurice Dupont settled quickly into Lir House. Within days we were calling him Maurice and he was coming and going about the place as he pleased, making himself coffee, taking glasses of wine into the sun. He told me one day that he was a widower and used to doing things his own way. He suited the mood of that summer in Lir House.

Liam's slaying of the bushes had revealed a long wooden table and garden seats that had been hidden. They faced the sea and when they were cleaned up they looked quite good. Maurice one day invited my grandmother to sit with him and it became a habit with them. She stuck resolutely to her daily Guinness while he had wine, and they seemed to get on well enough, even if Maurice did do most of the talking. She wore her black straw hat and he wore a pull-down cloth affair which looked a bit like a hanky. On the whole I preferred my grandmother's headgear.

Maurice very quickly found himself and his easel a spot on the lawn which gave him views both of the sea and house. I joined him there one hot afternoon, bringing my camera with me. He didn't seem to be doing much, just dabbling at a view of the headland, and he put his brush down as soon as I dropped to the grass beside him.

'What camera do you use?' he asked. I handed him the Pentax and he looked at it briefly, then handed it back.

'It's taken some good pictures.' I was immediately defensive.

'You have, *ma petite Martha*. The camera is only as good as the person who—' He took off the cloth hat and scratched his pate, frowning.

'Uses it?' I supplied, helpfully, and he put the hat back on again with a smile.

'Thank you, *ma petite*.'

Though I knew he called me this to distinguish me from my grandmother, whom he called Martha, it still made me feel good. Sort of small and cherished, things I'd never in my life felt before. He made Martha sound different too and for the first time in my life I liked the sound of my own name. I will always be grateful to him for that.

'And how are you going to use your camera today?'

He squinted out to sea as he said this. There was a boat moored close in.

'Don't know.' I didn't fancy the boat. 'Thought I'd have a look around and decide.'

'Try the boat,' Maurice suggested and I looked at it again.

The sea was so still that its sails were reflected, almost unmoving, across the water. 'It is not so very exciting a subject but it can teach you many things.'

He gave me a few tips and, because he seemed to know what he was talking about, I listened and then took a few shots. I did things his way and, even as I worked, knew that I had learned something.

I was right. The results, when I had the roll developed, were a lot better than I'd have managed on my own. I look at them sometimes and remember that day, before I knew about Maurice, and wonder at the person I was, at my innocence and ignorance.

Manus didn't return my call and I persuaded myself that his mother had forgotten to tell him I'd phoned.

I did get a letter from Naomi though, that week Maurice arrived. It was a paragraph long and left me wondering why she'd bothered to write at all. Dublin was boring, she said, and she hoped my grandmother wasn't 'an old cow'. That, more or less, was it. Nothing about Manus or what parties she'd been to or anything like that.

I shoved it back into the envelope and sat in my bedroom window to think about my answer. My thoughts surprised me. If my letter was to be honest I would have to admit to Naomi that there were things about my summer in the sticks that I quite liked. I would have to admit, for starters, that my grandmother was nothing like the old cow I'd expected her to be. That she accepted me as I was and didn't go on about everything, trying to change me.

There were other things too.

It was good to be able to leave my bedroom curtains open at night and let the sun, rising like a flaming mandarin over the sea, wake me in the mornings. Naomi wouldn't understand this but I knew myself, even then, that I would remember the sunrises of that summer for the rest of my life. And that I would forever compare them to other sunrises.

The only things in my new life which would interest Naomi were that I was getting a decent tan and that my hair was growing. This reduced my prospective letter to the same length as the one she'd sent me. In the end I decided not to write at all.

It had been sunny for so long that when the weather began to change it came as a shock. The first hint that all was not well was a hot, gusty wind. This blew up so suddenly that Maurice and I had to charge around after some of his drawing papers when it caught them.

'The weather is going to break. There's a storm on the way.' My grandmother, sitting at the garden table, studied the horizon. I followed her gaze and saw for myself how clouds were gathering.

'I hate storms,' I said.

'We need a good storm.' My grandmother was matter of fact. 'It'll freshen things up, clear the air a bit.'

'But I hate storms,' I said again. I meant it. For as long as I could remember thunder and lightning had truly terrified me. I crossed my fingers and touched wood that it wouldn't be a bad storm.

CHAPTER EIGHT

It was a dreadful storm. I went to bed with the window and curtains open as usual and woke around midnight to a three-pronged attack from thunder, lightning and a deluging rain which poured into the room. By the time I'd worked up the courage to get out of bed I had to walk through an inch of water to pull down the window.

I stood by the closed window, hypnotised by the horror of what was going on outside. My worst imaginings had come true and to save my life I couldn't move, not even to lift my feet from the pool of rainwater they were standing in. Lightning lit up the churning sea and bushes and trees as they thrashed about in the gale force wind. Rain beat with savage insistence against the window.

And still I stood there. I'd probably have spent the night by that window if there hadn't been a sudden lull. Then, like someone released from a trance I crept back to bed and buried myself under the blankets.

It was no good. As a ploy this had worked at home, during other storms. But home was a city, where there was protection and shelter everywhere. This was exposed, lonely, waiting-to-be-struck-by-lightning Lir House. I couldn't get the views from the window out of my head and when the wind began to build up again I almost fell out of bed and into my dressing gown. I knew I was being cowardly but I couldn't stay alone in that bedroom. I wanted my grandmother. I wanted her to tell me that the storm would pass over and not kill us all.

The doors along the corridor were rattling like crazy and I saw at once the my grandmother's was open. Her room was empty. I turned, saw a light in the hallway and realised she'd probably gone down to the kitchen. A sudden clap of thunder, sounding as if it was right overhead, propelled me headlong down the stairs. I had to be with her, wherever she was.

The kitchen door opened to the comforting smell of fresh coffee. My grandmother was there all right. She was sitting at the table with Maurice. I'd forgotten about Maurice. His hand held my grandmother's on the table and it looked as if the storm had shaken him badly too. Or it may have been the awful lighting in the kitchen that made his face look drawn, gave his eyes a flat darkness.

'I couldn't sleep.' My voice was squeaky. 'I came down for a drink.'

My grandmother stood at once. She didn't look great herself but just by being there she made things seem all right.

'Martha, my dear child.' She put an arm around me and led me to the table. 'Of course you couldn't sleep! How could you—how could *anyone* sleep through a storm like this one...' She put me sitting in a chair beside Maurice and, with her head to one side, looked at me closely.

'Maurice, bring a blanket from my room, will you please?' Her voice was sharp. 'You need a drink all right, my girl. Something hot.'

She began fussing at the cooker as Maurice, with a

quick pat to my hand, jumped out of his chair. Seconds later I heard him puttering up the stairs. He seemed to have got over his fear of the storm.

The wind was still howling outside, though in the kitchen it sounded further away. I began to shake. I couldn't stop myself. My feet were freeezing cold too, from standing on the sodden bedroom floor.

My grandmother muttered to herself by the cooker. Her hair was in a heavy plait almost to her waist and she was wearing a dark-blue dressing gown. Without her usual clutter of clothing you could see how bony she really was.

'I'm a selfish old woman.' She came back to the table and sat beside me in the chair vacated by Maurice. 'You told me you hated storms. I should have paid more attention. And now look at you, poor thing, cold and frightened.'

'I'm fine. It was just that the rain came in to the room. And then I could see it from the window, the lightning I mean.'

'You're not a bit fine.' Her voice was gruff. 'Older and wiser people than you have been frightened by the storms around Lir House. Only an unimaginative fool would be unaware of the danger.' She gave me a brief, hard hug. 'And you're not that.' She got up, poured some warm milk into a mug and placed it front of me. 'I want you to drink that,' she commanded, holding up a hand as I started to speak. 'Whether you like warm milk or not, drink it. There's nothing like it for the shivers.'

I drank. My grandmother noticed my bare feet and produced a pair of slippers from somewhere. Maurice, looking flustered, returned with an enormous blanket and together they wrapped it around me. I giggled. I couldn't seem to stop myself. I felt ridiculous and knew I looked it.

'That's better.' My grandmother spoke with satisfaction. 'You'll be fine now.' The three of us sat around the table and talked for what seemed like hours. My grandmother regaled us with stories of other storms, of trees coming down and seas which brought giant rocks into the cove below the cliff. Lir House had withstood them all, she said, and would withstand many more. Maurice told us about the people of the village he'd grown up in and where he'd now returned in retirement. He was very funny and the light had come back to his eyes.

I mostly listened. The pair of them seemed so much to enjoy talking about the past that I hadn't the heart to interrupt. At some point the storm died without my even noticing.

It was after three when my grandmother looked at the wall clock. 'It'll be a fine day,' she said. 'But breezy and cool. A day for walking, shaking off the cobwebs. We all need a bit of sleep now.'

She was right about its being good walking weather. I woke up early and full of energy. Around mid-morning I took myself off, on foot, to the village. It was an good hour's walk but I felt really invigorated when I got there. I'd brought my camera, in case I came across anything that would make a half-decent picture, and I walked through Faylinn slowly, looking at things. Somehow I found myself outside the supermarket, waving at Lorcan O'Neill as he stacked shelves. A girl of about my own age sat at the cash register. I beckoned him to come out and to my surprise he did.

'Your grandmother with you?' He looked up the street.

'No. I'm all on my own. Fancy a Coke, or something?' I jerked my head toward the pub and, after the shocked look left his face, he grinned.

'If you're buying.'

He gave a signal to the girl in the supermarket and we crossed the road to the pub I'd been in with my grandmother. My mother's old friend was there and served us the pint of rock shandy I wanted for myself and the beer Lorcan asked for.

'It's peace then, is it?' He raised his glass to me, caught my gaze and held it. I nodded and we clinked glasses. Since the Saturday of the trip-that-never-was to Wexford I'd hardly spoken to him at all and had neatly avoided helping with the dinner on several evenings.

'Peace,' I said and we drank to it.

'Maybe you'll let me tell you now what happened that day?' he asked. 'There really was nothing I could do, you know.'

'Right,' I said. 'Let's have it...'

'It was family stuff, as usual. My sister, that's her over in the shop, arrived home from London that morning. She wasn't expected—first thing we knew about it was when she rang from Wexford, asking me to collect her from the station.' He pulled a face. 'Big brothers are conveniences, as far as she's concerned. Anyway, I figured I'd just about make it there and back in time to pick you up. And I would have too except that when I got to the station she wasn't there. She'd buzzed off with this friend of hers. It took me forty minutes to find her, another ten to sort out a situation with the friend. That was a mistake. While we were collecting her bags at the station he did a job on the tank of my bike. The result was that before we were half way home I ran out of juice. Miles from a phone, already late to meet you.'

'I see,' I said, and I did. I absolutely believed him. It was much too convoluted a story to be a lie. 'Your sister?'

'Is being an almighty pain at the moment. She was supposed to stay with an aunt in London, work there for the summer. Only as soon as she'd earned the fare she got on a boat and came home.'

I had a flash of intuition. 'She was sent there because of this friend in Wexford, wasn't she?'

'Seemed like a good idea at the time.'

I could see he didn't want to talk about it but I wanted to know. 'Whose idea?'

'My mother's. Mine too, I suppose.'

'What age is your sister?'

He didn't look at me when he answered. 'Sixteen. But she's young for her age.'

'Says who? You? Lorcan, that was a real last-century way to deal with things, you know that? It's up to your sister herself to find out what the guy is like...'

He looked really uncomfortable. 'I hate to say it, but I think you're right. And it's looking like she's found out. He doesn't seem to be around anymore. Something to do with him doing the job on my tank.' We were quiet for a while and then he said, 'Emer's helping with the shop since she came back. Gives me a bit of free time. Like now. We can go to Wexford today if you like.'

I liked. I rang my grandmother and we went straight away. I wore the red helmet and felt free as the wind as we zipped along the road. When we got to the town centre Lorcan locked the bike and we wandered about for a bit. It was noisy and crowded with narrow, shady streets running off at angles, under arches and up hills. I liked it and was glad I'd brought my camera. In no time at all I'd got several shots I felt really good about.

It got warmer and when we came to an ice-cream parlour I began to drool. We bought a couple of gigantic cones and went down to the sea and sat on a wall watching boats while we ate them.

'My grandmother says you're going to Switzerland in September,' I said.

'That's the plan anyway.' He got all wound up, became like a different person as he told about the course he was going to do, about how he wasn't going to be just any old chef. He was going to be one of the best and he was going to cook in the world's top restaurants.

'I owe a lot to your grandmother.' He looked at me seriously. 'She went guarantor for me and gave me the summer job so that I could get experience before going.'

'She says she gave you the job because you're good.'

'There's that too.' He gave a conceited grin. 'But I still owe her. Mind you, she's always been decent about summer jobs. Half the people in the village have worked in Lir House at one time or another. In the years when it was busy, that is.'

This, my grandmother as the local Lady Bountiful, was an angle I hadn't thought about. I wondered, and not for the first time, what she would do and where she would go when she sold the hotel in the autumn.

We finished the ice-creams and were quiet for a while, in a comfortable sort of way. Then a breeze blew up and Lorcan took my hand. 'Let's go,' he said.

We walked back through the town holding hands and I noticed how girls looked at him as we passed. I just felt very relaxed. Lorcan was a mate. Or at least he was becoming one.

He became a bit more in the week which followed. It just happened. It was all to do with the summer, the return of the sunshine and Lorcan's new-found free time. My grandmother and Maurice were getting on well and this made it easy to take off in the afternoons for a good sandy swimming beach Lorcan knew. The second day we went there we stayed a long time in the water and the place was deserted by the time we got out.

We were quite alone when Lorcan kissed me. It took me completely by surprise. One minute I was kneeling there, drying myself and laughing at some rubbish he was going on about. The next minute I was being kissed.

And then just as suddenly he stopped kissing me. 'Got to get to work.' he jumped up, pulling me with him.

I felt awful, awkward, embarrassed. I tried desperately for cool. 'Mustn't keep the boss waiting.' I laughed, bent my head as I towelled off the sand, pulled on my T-shirt. When my burning cheeks had cooled down I straightened up again and faced him.

He held out a hand and I took it as we walked across the sand.

We were climbing the steps up from the beach when we met Judy Moore. If I'd known then what I know about her now I wouldn't have been so pleasant when Lorcan introduced us. In fact I wouldn't have spoken to her at all. She was with another girl, whom she didn't bother to introduce, and she asked how the water was.

'Great.' Lorcan was quite curt and not inclined to stop. She moved just enough to block our way.

'Aren't you going to introduce us?' She nodded at me and smiled sweetly. Or so I thought.

'This is Martha.' Lorcan's voice was flat. 'Martha, this is Judy Moore.' He made another attempt to move on but Judy Moore seemed not to notice that she was blocking the way. She went into the social comedy about being delighted to meet me.

'Your grandmother is Lir House, isn't she?'

This seemed to me an odd but accurate enough way of putting it so I said yes.

'Lucky you, having Lorcan as your private chef all summer. Though I hear there aren't too many guests up there.'

'No. My grandmother is winding things down. It's her last season.'

'How convenient. That must give you all plenty of free time.'

She flashed a look Lorcan's way and warning bells began to ring in my head at last.

'I've got a job to do, Judy. See ⎯⎯⎯⎯ ⎯⎯⎯ und.' Lorcan made another move but she ⎯⎯⎯ ⎯⎯ und as if rooted.

'Funny you haven't been ⎯⎯⎯⎯ ⎯⎯ r House before.' She stared pointedly at ⎯⎯ ⎯⎯ vhich had

78

erupted on my chin that morning. 'Your grandmother's been alone up there for years. I never heard
of any family visiting before.'

'I was here as a child...'

'Oh were you really? Not since then?'

'Excuse us, Judy.' Lorcan took my hand and made
his request very pointedly. She smiled at him and did a
funny little skip sideways.

'See you around, Lorcan,' Judy Moore called as we
passed. 'You too Martha.'

Lorcan pulled at my hand impatiently when I
looked back. I said nothing as we climbed to the field
where we'd left the bike but, once I had my head
inside the helmet, felt safe enough about asking a
question.

'Does your friend Judy come from the village?'

'She's not my friend.' He was revving up the engine
so I had to strain to hear him. 'Not a particular friend
anyway. Not any longer.'

This was all I wanted to know. I settled quite
happily on my seat on the pillion. I even hummed to
myself as we buzzed along the road to Lir House.

Going through the village I noticed that posters
announcing the annual visit of a fun-fair had been
plastered all over the place. It might be good crack; I
would suggest to Lorcan that we go together. The
prospect cheered me up even further.

CHAPTER NINE

After that day I became caught up in the summer's mood and stopped hoping every phone call to Lir House was for me. I gave up on letters too and just lazed along, happy to let things happen. So it was, that when the phone rang early one morning a week later, I only vaguely wondered if it could be for me. Even when my grandmother called I took my time making my way downstairs.

It was quite a surprise to hear Naomi on the line. The first thing that occurred to me was that something must be up for her to ring so early in the day.

'You still alive down there?' she asked. I began to gabble a bit, about why I hadn't written and how the summer was turning out OK. She cut me short. 'No time to gossip, Martha. My mother's hassling me about the phone. Listen, I'm planning a trip down to see you.'

She paused to take in my gratified response but all I felt was a curious heart flop. This, the realisation that I didn't really want Naomi to come, came as a complete shock to me. While I tried to understand my reaction a silence lengthened on the line. Naomi broke it. 'Are you still there Martha? Did you hear what I said?'

'Yes. That's great news, Naomi. When are you thinking of coming?'

Even to my own ears I didn't sound enthusiastic. I wasn't surprised when she got annoyed. 'Well! I'm certainly not coming if I'm not welcome! You don't

80

sound as if you want me there at all.'

'Of course I do! Don't be daft, Naomi.'

To make up for my lack of enthusiasm I put a lot of energy into my reply. 'You took me by surprise, that's all. You *know* you're not exactly the country type.'

'For you I'm willing to make the ultimate sacrifice,' she giggled. 'How about if I came down next weekend? It's dead boring around here. My parents won't let me do *anything*. But I know they'll let me off the leash if it's to visit you and your gran.' She giggled again. 'I could be there on Saturday.'

'Terrif. I'll meet you from the train.' This seemed the least I could do.

'No. I mean you may not have to.' Naomi became breathlessly hurried. 'I'm working on a plan. How'd you like to see Manus as well? Two for the price of one?' The heart flop thing happened again. This time Naomi rattled on over my silence. 'He's using his mother's car a lot these days. How about if I persuade him to drive me down? I think I can do it.'

'His mother's car?' I played for time.

'It's not such a big deal.' Naomi was impatient. 'Anyway, I'll see you sometime on Saturday, *with* lover boy. Just leave it to me. Hope the hotel's not booked out.'

'No. It's not. Look, Naomi, I haven't heard from Manus and—'

'Don't worry. I've been talking to him. He thinks about you a *lot*. Tell you all on Saturday. I've got to go now, my mother's being a real pain about this phone. Bye-eee.'

'Bye.'

I put the phone down and sat looking at it. What

was wrong with me? Naomi was my best friend and I adored Manus. So why wasn't I leaping about the place with joy?

I went outside to see the morning. A mist was drifting slowly across the headland and out to sea. I could see another sunny day taking shape. It would be lazy, comfortable. My grandmother would make breakfast and, later on, Maurice and I would make lunch. Things had somehow developed that way. My grandmother had slowed down and was taking things easy in a way I felt sure she'd never done before. She had sent again for Liam to cut the grass but even he was taking his time about coming. A pleasant, midsummer torpor seemed to be affecting everyone.

That afternoon Lorcan was going to take me to Wexford to collect a roll of film. And on Saturday I would be going to the funfair in the village with him. On Saturday...But on Saturday Manus would be here. I began to feel slightly sick. It was exactly the nauseous feeling you get when you're waiting to be interviewed by a teacher at school, or opening an exam result envelope. What was I to tell Lorcan? How would I explain Manus to him? On the other hand, why should I tell him anything? Lorcan and I were just friends, after all. There was no need to tell him *everything* about my life.

I kicked at the gravel. My grandmother would yell if she saw me but I didn't car. I kicked at it for a good while; then went inside for my breakfast.

Things were still confused in my head when I went to bed that night. Naomi, I knew, would laugh at my life in Lir House. Manus would find it dead boring. Much as I cared for both of them, and much and long as I'd wanted Manus to come, I knew they wouldn't fit in. They weren't Lir House people. It wasn't their fault; it was just a fact of life.

In the days which followed the problem got worse. I couldn't bring myself to tell anyone about the expected visit. Supposing I did and then they didn't show? If that happened I'd have put myself, as well as my grandmother and Lorcan, through a lot of unnecessary hassle.

My parents rang but the subject of Manus was not even breathed. There would be sheer hysteria if my mother discovered he was to be a weekend visitor to Lir House. With any luck, if he did come, my mother might never find out. Naomi wouldn't say anything and I couldn't see my grandmother telling her either.

Which of course brought me to another problem. What exactly was I to tell my grandmother about Manus? I knew instinctively that, while she might disagree with my mother on everything else, she would agree with her on the subject of Manus. She would not like him. She would be absolutely courteous because she was like that, but she wouldn't like him. I was surprised how much this mattered to me.

By Thursday I was feeling really tense about Saturday. In the morning I sat with Maurice as he painted but felt too edgy to pay much attention to his anecdotes and chat. He knew it too. 'You are preoccupied, *ma chère*,' he said gently. 'Maybe you should tell Maurice what is on your mind?'

I shook my head. He was painting the house. He hadn't got it exactly right yet but he was getting there. I jumped up.

'I'm going for a swim.' I gave him a kiss on the

cheek, to show I wasn't being rude, and belted off to the cove. I had a second swim later, with Lorcan, on a beach that was new to me. We held hands a lot and had a great deal of fun but Lorcan hadn't kissed me again. Which was just as well, considering the confused state I was in. That day we went back to Lir House early. Lorcan wanted time to cook something Maurice had especially asked for.

And still I didn't tell him about Manus. Or about Naomi. How could I tell about one without mentioning the other?

As soon as he got into the kitchen Lorcan began to get all worked up about getting Maurice's *Poulet au Riz à la Creme* just right. I should have stayed out of his way but I didn't. When things started to go wrong at the sauce stage he snapped at me to stop picking the cooked chicken.

'I'm hungry,' I protested and took another piece.

'Then eat something else. Here.' Her threw me an apple which I caught and began to nibble. That was when the sauce boiled over. Not my fault, of course, but Lorcan got really mad at me anyway. 'Martha! If you want to mess about then do it somewhere else.'

He pulled the saucepan off the cooker, slammed it furiously into the sink. I had the awful feeling that I was going to cry. I didn't want him shouting at me. I wanted him to forget the *poulet* and rice and to sit down so that I could talk to him and tell him about Manus coming on Saturday. This was unreasonable and stupid and made me angry with myself and with him too because he couldn't see that I was upset.

'Right!' I yelled. 'I'm going. You can play the prima donna chef on your own! And don't put any of your creation on a plate for me! I won't be having dinner.'

'Fine!' He began melting butter to begin the sauce again. He didn't even look up when I left.

I didn't go down to dinner. I made an excuse to my grandmother and Maurice about not feeling well. They looked quite worried, not knowing what was wrong and only half believing me, I could tell. I didn't like lying to them but having taken my stand in the kitchen I couldn't very well back down. As fights go it had been more of a squabble—but it had made it absolutely impossible to explain to Lorcan about Manus.

I was sitting by my window when he roared away on the bike. I was still sitting there when my grandmother and Maurice toddled down the garden path together. They did this every evening, walking as far as the cliff's edge and back. Afterwards, on warm evenings like this one, they would have coffee at the table in the garden. It was all very sedate.

I watched idly as they stood looking at the darkening blue of the sea and sky. They made a comical picture, my grandmother like an overdressed scarecrow, Maurice as neatly turned out as a soldier.

They were on their way back to the house when my grandmother, quite suddenly, stopped still and closed her eyes. She stood, absolutely rigid, saying something to Maurice. He put an arm around her and she leaned against him. I felt my mouth go dry. What could be wrong with her?

Maurice seemed to be coping so I stayed where I was, for the moment. He tried to encourage her to walk on but she shook her head. He put both arms around her then and held her, his stick dangling. She put her head on his shoulder and they stood like that for a while.

They were a picture. I reached for my camera and took it. Months later, when I could bring myself to get it developed, the picture had nothing of the sense of how they were that evening, none of the fearful sadness I'd felt watching them. I had a lot to learn about photography. And even more to learn about people.

After a little while my grandmother lifted her head and they started to walk slowly towards the house again. They sat at the wooden table and faced the sea. From the window I could hear the low murmur of their voices.

I went downstairs to make their coffee.

CHAPTER TEN

They didn't hear me coming across the grass. My grandmother looked up and smiled in surprise when I put the coffee things on the table. As smiles go it wasn't a howling success.

'Thank you, Martha,' she said. 'Are you feeling better?'

I fiddled about with the business of pouring and tried not to look at her again. I'd never seen her look quite so *old* before. Even her voice had aged.

'There was nothing wrong with me,' I admitted as I put a cup in front of her. 'What about you, though? I saw you on the path.'

'Oh, that.' my grandmother took a sip of her coffee. 'Just a little turn. At my age one can't expect all the parts to work as well as they used to. Bits and pieces of the body let you down from time to time. It's nothing to worry about.'

'Has it happened to you before then?'

As my grandmother hesitated, Maurice, with a small cough, tapped the side of his cup.

'You have left me without coffee, *ma petite*,' he said. I filled his cup and was about to tackle my grandmother again when he put a hand gently over mine. 'Your grandmother is tired,' he said.

'Really, it's nothing to worry about,' she assured me. And with that I had to be content. It was obvious they were pulling the rank of old age on me.

It would have been discreet, and kind, to go away

and leave them alone then. But a wormy devil of curiosity was at work in me and I stayed where I was, dropping into the third seat at the table.

'You are not hungry yet?' Maurice asked. I shook my head.

He watched me over the rim of his coffee cup. I couldn't quite decide what his expression meant. It looked quite serious.

'I would like to make your picture, *ma petite Martha*.' He spoke just as I was beginning to fidget. 'I will start it now, this evening.'

He wasn't so much asking as telling me, but in a nice way.

'OK.' I sat up, grinning. 'How do you want me to pose?'

'First, I would like you to go to my room and bring me my drawing block and pencils. Then we will think about how you must sit.'

Once in Maurice's room I took a good look around. My grandmother had insisted on looking after his bedlinen so I hadn't been into the room since he moved in. It looked quite different from when Ron and Mabel had stayed there, very different from when Otto had been its occupant. Maurice had changed the bed so that it faced the window and had pinned quite a few of his watercolours on the walls. There were books and magazines everywhere.

I found the drawing block and pencils quite quickly. It occurred to me that I should bring an eraser too, but I couldn't see one anywhere. I was crossing to the window, thinking I would call down to Maurice, when I saw the chest. It was open by the side of the bed and was full of watercolours. I couldn't resist having a look.

The top picture was unfamiliar so I took it out to give it a closer inspection. It was of Lir House, but quite different from anything I'd seen Maurice paint that summer.

The colours were darker, for one thing, and he'd been heavy-handed with the paint in a way he wasn't usually. But the signature was his, bold and clear in the right-hand corner. So it had to be his. Perhaps he was trying for a different technique in the dark of the midnight hours.

I took the picture to the window, along with a few of the others, to have a look in the stronger light. When I studied it properly I saw that it wasn't just the painting style which was different. Lir House itself didn't look the same. There was a lot less ivy for one thing. And the garden had bushes and flowers that were definitely not there now. The other pictures were of Lir House and the cliff top as well, all views I'd seen Maurice working on. But they too looked *different*.

The reason came to even before I turned one over to check for a date. These weren't the pictures Maurice had painted in the last few weeks! He'd painted them on his earlier visit to Lir House.

The date on the first picture I turned over came as a shock. It was inscribed from Maurice to my grandmother and had been painted on 18 July 1946. A lifetime ago! Maurice had never said his previous visit had been so far in the past. No reason why he should, of course, but you'd expect him at least to have mentioned it. Or to have made the usual comparisons about how things had changed, that sort of thing. He behaved, instead, as if only a couple of summers had gone by since his last visit.

I looked again at the first picture.

So *that* was how Lir House had been forty-five years ago. It had aged well. I went through the other pictures in the chest and it was as if I was putting a whole summer through my hands. There were sunrise and evening watercolours, bright and dark ones. Maurice must have spent quite a while at Keshkorran in 1946.

Half way down the chest the pictures began to change. Now they were of French country scenes, rivers and woods mostly. There were a lot of them and they were dated from 1947 until a few months ago.

I put back the French pictures and gathered up the ones of Lir House.

Then I went downstairs to find out what it was all about.

CHAPTER ELEVEN

This time Maurice and my grandmother were waiting for me as I came across the grass. They watched silently as I approached with the pictures in my hand.

I put them on the table between us and sat facing them.

'I didn't meant to be rude,' I said to Maurice, 'but the chest was open and I couldn't resist having a look. You never said it was forty-five years since you last stayed here.'

Maurice picked up the top picture. He didn't smile or say a word as he looked at it. He picked up a second one and gave it the silent scrutiny treatment too, this time with a small smile. He handed it to my grandmother.

'I painted this the first week I came,' he said, 'when I could not sleep. The sunrises gave me such pleasure.'

She took the picture out of his hand and held it away, looking at it. It was of a fully risen, flaming sun.

'I remember. I was afraid you would become ill again when I saw you outside, painting so early in the morning.'

Maurice, who had picked up another picture, made a very French tut-tutting sound. 'Too much paint. Not enough water. This is carelessly done.' He picked up others, handing them one by one to my grandmother with a comment each. 'But I improved, did I not? The August ones are better.'

'Very much better.' My grandmother took the

pictures from him, looking indulgently at each. Her voice, normally so matter-of-fact, was gentle and a little sad. But by then I'd had enough of feeling like an exclusion zone.

'Hello!' I waved my hand in the air. 'Remember me?'

Maurice went on looking at the pictures but my grandmother turned my way. 'You must excuse us, Martha. Nostalgia is a vice of old age.' She smiled at Maurice, who handed her the last picture from the pile.

'You could at least share it. Tell me something about the summer of 1946. What was it like here then? It was so long ago. My mother wasn't even born...'

'It was quiet,' said Maurice. 'But not so very different. And there were more guests than this summer. The war had just ended and people were beginning to live without fear.'

'Why did you come to such a quiet place?'

'Because quiet, *ma chère*, and above all peace, were what I wanted. I had been injured in the war.' He tapped his leg. 'When they released me from the hospital the doctors said I needed to rest my head as well as my leg. An Irish doctor gave me the address of Lir House and I so I came. The air was clean and your grandmother was kind to me. I recovered and returned to France, to my family, *et voilà*!' He told all this quite quickly. When he'd finished he put the pictures neatly together and stood up. 'The light has changed. I will wait until tomorrow to begin making your picture, ma *petite*. *Aussi*, your grandmother needs a rest.'

He held out an arm to her but my grandmother shook her head.

'No, Maurice,' she said. 'We will talk a little more. I

think it is time to put some things to rights.' She held out a hand and Maurice, after a small hesitation, took it. He kissed her fingertips lightly and sat down again, holding her hand as she began to speak. 'We've come a long way from that summer, my dear old friend.' She turned to me. 'And you, Martha, have a long, long way to go. You should go through life with the truth.'

She turned back to Maurice and they exchanged a look. At that moment it became blindingly clear to me how much they cared for each other. I couldn't believe I hadn't noticed it before. Something else, too, was beginning to dawn on me.

'Look,' I began desperately, 'you don't have to tell me your business. I'd no right. Your past is your own; it belongs to both of you. You don't have to share it with me.'

'But we do.' My grandmother's voice was firm. 'We must. I see that now. I didn't before. And you are old enough to know, even though your mother will not be pleased.'

She looked away, out to sea. She was wearing her straw hat and it shadowed her eyes. I would have liked very much to see them. I saw Maurice squeeze her hand but he didn't say anything. After a while my grandmother turned to me again. 'You are not like your mother, Martha. You are a different generation and you are stronger, in many ways. You are less frightened. But your mother helped make you those things; you must never forget that.'

It didn't seem a time for disagreement so I stayed silent. My grandmother took a deep breath and began, in her raspy voice, to tell me the story of her life, and of my mother's life. It was the story of Maurice too.

'I was looking after Lir House on my own when Maurice arrived here at the beginning of July, 1946. My parents had died some years before and, because I couldn't bear to part with the family home, I had started running Lir House as a hotel. I was twenty-eight and had never had time for the things of girlhood—boys, dances, all of that. I didn't mind. Lir House was my life, even then. Maurice arrived in a taxi with a suitcase and his easel. He had no booking but I was very glad to have a French guest who was willing to stay the whole summer. Especially one I was convinced was a war hero.'

'A bad-tempered ex-soldier.' Maurice interrupted. 'I was very bad-tempered.'

'Yes. You were bad-tempered at first. But you were in distress, anyone could see that. He was not a good patient, Martha. Few men are. After a few days he began to paint and his health and mood improved remarkably. He said he felt "at home" in Lir House. We became friends. After a little while we became lovers too.'

She stopped. I think she wanted to be sure I understood what she was saying. I understood all right. It all seemed perfectly logical, even if I had difficulty imagining Maurice and my grandmother in the throes of a grand passion. She went on, more slowly,

'We created a private world, spent a great deal of time together. But by September, as the summer ended, reality took over. Maurice had a wife and child in France. He had married at the outbreak of war, gone underground soon after. We both knew that his responsibilities were to his family, that it was out of the question for him to stay here. Our love affair was something which had happened because time, place and circumstances had brought us together. It would not have been right to make it the cause of suffering to others. We agreed to exchange letters, as friends do. We would allow ourselves that much at least. Maurice left in the second week of September and by the end of that month I realised I was pregnant. Your mother was born the following April.'

My head spun. I sat and stared mutely, at her, at Maurice. There was so much I wanted to say that it all became a jumble in my head and I couldn't get the words together. I had the awful feeling I was going to cry and then Maurice, exactly as he had done with my grandmother on the path, came round the table and put his arms around me.

'I am proud and happy that you are my grandchild,' he said.

That did it. I really cried then.

But not for long. What, after all, was there to cry about? I had discovered a grandfather, and that my mother was a love-child. You couldn't exactly call the situation tragic, or say that it represented the end of life as I knew it.

It was merely the end of living a lie.

Maurice took his arm away, handed me a big hanky and went back to sitting beside my grandmother. I straightened up, blew my nose and looked across the table at the pair of them. They were my *grandparents*— and the fact didn't seem at all strange. Over the weeks I'd got used to thinking of them as a couple. I felt easy in their company. In many ways a lot easier than I did with my parents.

'So, what happened then?' I demanded. 'When did you tell Maurice he was to be a father? And why does my mother think he's dead?'

My grandmother sighed, stiffened a little. I could see her square her shoulders as she got down to the nitty-gritty.

'Maurice wrote to me, as he'd promised, and I replied. But your mother was two years old before I told him of her existence. I had known what a terrible conflict it would cause him, you see. But it took me a while to realise I was doing him a grave injustice by not telling him about his child. When I did at last write and tell him he immediately wanted to come. I wouldn't hear of it. I knew that I was quite capable of rearing our child alone. Any other solution would have caused a great deal of unhappiness to many people.'

'But he did come, at least to visit?' It seemed incomprehensible to me that Maurice had never seen his daughter.

'He has never visited until now. I would not permit it.'

This did shock me. I thought of all those years, forty-five of them since my mother was born, and of my grandmother and Maurice never seeing each other. I thought that my grandmother was very stubborn, very sure that she was right. And I thought that, in her whole life, my mother had never seen her father.

Or had she? Maybe she'd been to France and not told me?

Maurice took up the story so I didn't have to ask about this.

'It was not easy,' he said, 'never to see my child. But in time I accepted the decision of your *grandmère*. We wrote, always. And every summer, wherever I was, I painted little watercolours for her. At Christmas she would allow me to send some wine.'

'Too much wine,' my grandmother said. 'You always sent far too much wine, Maurice. But those things,' she turned to me again, 'were just signs of friendship. Later, when I decided to send Jane away to school, it was Maurice who paid for her education.'

'But why did my mother tell me her father was dead?'

'Because, as a child growing up, that is what she believed. That is what I *allowed* her to believe. When she was very small and began to ask questions about her father I told her he had gone away. She assumed I meant to heaven and I left it at that. It was wrong of me. Very wrong. But I didn't realise it at the time. I should have told her the truth and I should have foreseen what would happen. She was thirteen when she heard the local gossip about me, from a group of cruel and jeering children at school. We had been very close until then and she felt I had totally betrayed her. She had trusted me and I had lied to her. She felt betrayed too by the father who had left her.'

I could believe all this. I'd have felt the same myself, if I'd discovered at thirteen that my mother had been lying to me for my whole life. Even without any particular reason, my mother and I had stopped getting on when I was thirteen. It's a bad age.

'Did you tell her then who her father was?'

'No, and that was wrong too. She was so angry, you see. I was afraid that if I told her his name, and where he was, she would do something destructive. I seriously feared she would get in touch with Maurice's family. I explained as well as I could, and told her that her father cared very much for her. But of course it wasn't enough and she never understood. Never. She said she wanted to go away, to boarding school, and in the end I decided it might be the best thing. I was wrong about that too. I should not have allowed her to go, not to the school she chose anyway.

'It was a very proper convent school and in those days it was a harsh environment for a girl whose background was different. And my poor Jane wanted so passionately to be the same as everyone else. She told her friends I was a widow and in time, I am convinced, came to believe the lie.

'She was ashamed of me and tried to keep me away on open days at school. She couldn't understand either why I kept Lir House on. It was lonely, she said, and cold. If I sold we could move where no one knew us.'

My grandmother looked up at the long windows of Lir House. I looked at the encroaching ivy.

'We had many rows about this old house. I couldn't bring myself to sell. I wouldn't have known how to live anywhere else. Eventually she met your father and set about creating her own respectability. A proper family. She visited, at first. But as soon as you and Garrett became old enough to ask questions she stopped coming. I lost her completely then.'

Her voice had become tired and she stopped. A long silence developed and during it I experienced a deep sorrow for both my mother and grandmother. I ended it by saying, 'Things'll be different now. Me being here has sort of broken the ice, hasn't it? I'll ask Garrett to come down, and Dad, and she'll have to come with them.'

'No!' My grandmother gave a hoarse cry and Maurice reached out a calming hand. I was upset myself. As a plan to bring the family together my idea seemed all right to me. It didn't seem fair of my grandmother to reject it out of hand.

'Have you a better idea?' I was a bit short.

'There's something else you don't know, Martha.' My grandmother sighed. 'Your mother imposed a condition on your staying here for the summer. I was not to tell you about your grandfather. I agreed and you came here on those terms. Maybe I have done wrong again, in telling you now.'

She sighed again and fell silent. I could see that all of this was taking a lot out of her but I couldn't not say what I was thinking.

'But she's done to me, and to Garrett too, what she hated you for doing to her. She let us live with a lie.'

'Yes. It's not true, Martha, that we learn from our mistakes. Not true at all.' My grandmother tried a smile. It almost worked.

Another question came to me. There was no end to them, to what I needed to know. 'But what about Maurice? You must have known he was coming too. Did you not think that I would find out?'

'I didn't know definitely that Maurice was coming until his letter arrived. Over the years we had both come to accept that we would never meet again. It had even come to seem the best thing. Then, when I decided to close the hotel, I wrote to Maurice asking if he would like to visit for a couple of weeks. I knew his wife was dead and I hoped, but did not believe, that he would come. And I hoped too, but did not believe, that Jane would allow you to visit for the summer. I told myself that if you both arrived then it would be because fate had decided you should meet. It would not really be of my doing.' She stopped and no one said anything until she went on again. 'I still believe that fate has had a lot to do with bringing the two of you here this summer.'

She nodded her head, more to herself than anyone else, and got slowly to her feet. When she wobbled a bit Maurice was immediately by her side. Her hair had come loose at the back and she held his arm with one hand as she tried to fix it.

'Here, let me do it,' I said and she turned around, obediently. She still held on to Maurice who watched silently as I fiddled around, piling her hair back up under the hat.

'I think,' my grandmother said, 'that we should let fate work out the rest of the summer. We will find a way to tell Jane, I'm sure of it.'

Maurice said nothing. He was being very quiet.

'It's getting dark,' my grandmother said. Surprised, I saw that she was right. The sky had become rose-streaked and the rhododenderons darkly massed along the avenue. The midges were out too and my arms and legs began to itch.

I led the way inside, my grandmother following on Maurice's arm.

CHAPTER TWELVE

It was late when we went to bed but even so I couldn't sleep. I wished I had someone to talk to, someone who wasn't involved. It would have to be someone who knew my grandmother and Maurice, but was outside the 'situation'. Which meant, of course, that it would have to be Lorcan. He was the only possible person I could tell. I wished with all my heart that I hadn't rowed with him.

In the morning there was only myself and Maurice for breakfast. My grandmother was having what he called a *'grasse matinée'*, what I insisted was a lie-in. I went for a swim about mid-morning and, when I was coming back, saw him disappear down the avenue in a taxi. Feeling a bit peeved he hadn't offered to take me with him, I decided to walk down to the village myself anyway. It would give me a chance to clear up last evening's row with Lorcan. Maybe then I could talk to him about all that had happened.

Lorcan was serving a customer when I went into the supermarket. She was a real old biddy and she was giving him a hard time about the way he was cutting the cheese. Nothing he did pleased her. I was grinning away, adding to his discomfort, when she turned on me too.

'Have you nothing to do but stand there, smirking like a chimpanzee?' she demanded. 'A big strong girl like you! Take hold of those bags over there and carry them to the car outside for me. Go on now.'

I didn't have the nerve to refuse so I picked up the bags of groceries.

The car was a spanking new Volvo and the driver was eighty if he was a day. I wouldn't have put him in charge of a wheelbarrow. He didn't even look at me when I put the bags in the back seat. The woman came out and was barely into the car before he took off down the street like a bat out of hell. I closed my eyes and waited for the sound of a crash but it didn't come.

The episode nicely broke the ice with Lorcan. He was the one smirking like an chimpanzee when I went back into the shop. I sniffed, tossing my hair elegantly back. It was growing quickly in the sun and I'd washed it before coming out. Nothing to do with impressing Lorcan, of course.

He called his sister Emer to take over the shop for a while. She was a bit iffy about it but agreed when he promised to intercede to have her allowed go to the fun-fair. We went across the road to the pub and I gave him an abbreviated account of everything I'd learned the evening before. He was looking thoughtful when I finished.

'You know,' he said. 'I'm not really all that surprised. I always thought she was a woman with a past. But Maurice being your grandfather—now *that* is something else.' He was quiet for a while and I let him get used to the idea. 'She'd never have got away with keeping it secret, you know,' He said eventually. 'One of the old people in the village would have twigged and the gossip would have started again.'

'I don't think she thought it could be kept secret. She believes fate has brought Maurice and me together here this summer.'

'Good old fate,' Lorcan grinned. 'How does it feel anyway, suddenly finding a grandfather?'

'Weird, but nice.

We didn't talk much more because Lorcan had to go back to the shop. But I felt really glad I'd told him. It made the situation manageable somehow.

I was on my way back to Lir House when the other thing I should have told Lorcan bounced into my head. The fun-fair was going up in the field. It was to open the next day, Saturday. New, screaming posters promised it would be 'The Biggest and Best Night of the Summer.' My grandmother's revelations had temporarily pushed it, and the Manus factor, right out of my mind.

I would *have* to tell Lorcan that evening. My grandmother too. And Maurice. It wouldn't be fair not to tell him. I wondered idly if he would like me to call him Grandfather. On balance I decided not.

It was lunchtime when I got back to Lir House. My grandmother and Maurice weren't in the dining room, as they usually were. They weren't in the kitchen either. I was crossing the hall when Maurice came softly down the stairs, motioning me to be quiet.

'Your grandmother is sleeping,' he said.

He looked a bit tired himself, which was understandable. A late night, coupled with the strain of bringing a long-kept secret into the open, would tire anyone.

'I'm going to make myself something to eat,' I said. 'Will I get you something too?'

He watched as I made us sandwiches, seeming a bit preoccupied. We ate together in the kitchen. It wasn't until afterwards, in my room, that I remembered the taxi and wondered why Maurice hadn't mentioned where he'd been that morning. He hadn't gone to the village or I'd have seen him there. Maybe he didn't want me to know about his little outing. Everyone, after all, was entitled to their little secrets.

Because she was on my mind I wrote to my mother. I made the letter as friendly as I could, telling her that my swimming had improved and that I was learning to cook a bit. I said nothing about Maurice or about Manus. So in a way you could say that I told her nothing at all. Even so, I felt I'd done something positive. As if I'd held out a hand to her.

Everything went sickeningly wrong with my plan to tell Lorcan about Manus that evening. My grandmother appeared in the late afternoon announcing that she was *too* rested and insisting that she would help Lorcan prepare dinner. I couldn't explain Manus to Lorcan while she was there. It didn't help my digestion at dinner either, knowing I was going to have to explain to him after I'd finished eating.

Only that didn't happen either. Half way through dinner I heard the bike roar off down the avenue.

'Lorcan has to take his sister somewhere,' my grandmother explained. 'I told him to leave early.'

'I don't believe it!' My wail was involuntary so of course they wanted to know what was wrong. Explaining meant I finally told my grandmother and Maurice, at least, about the next day's visitors. I made very light of it but I could see they knew something was up.

'How long will they stay?' my grandmother asked.

I mumbled a bit. This was something Naomi hadn't

mentioned. 'A few hours. Well, maybe overnight.'

'They'll need to be fed then,' my grandmother was brisk. 'And I'll make up a couple of beds just in case.'

It was Maurice who sussed the reason I'd been slow to tell Lorcan.

'Are they a *couple*, your friends?' he asked. I pretended not to understand and tried a puzzled face. My grandmother was having none of it.

'Are they boyfriend and girlfriend, Martha?' She asked the question gently but insistently and I knew that she knew the answer.

'No,' I said miserably. 'They're not. Manus is my boyfriend. I'm not supposed to allow him come here. Naomi is my best friend.'

'*Oh, là là!*' It was the first time I'd actually heard Maurice say this and the very Frenchness of it almost made me giggle. Almost. He was looking very disapproving.

'It'll be all right, Maurice,' I assured him but he just frowned.

'We'll need some extra bits and pieces for dinner,' my grandmother said practically. 'I'll make a list and you can telephone Lorcan to get them together. It'll give you a chance to tell him too.'

'On the phone!' I was appalled.

'Better than not telling him at all,' my grandmother was firm.

When I telephoned a half-hour later Lorcan's mother answered. He was out, she said, and wouldn't be back until much later.

That left first thing in the morning. I would have to tell him then, or never.

On my way to bed I passed the wretched Fiachra on

the stairs. He was licking his paws and cleaning himself with undue satisfaction. I bent down and we eyeballed each other.

'You'll get yours,' I hissed, 'one of these days.' He didn't even blink.

The next morning was cloudy, but warm and promising sun later. I washed my hair, again, and was looking in the mirror, trying to do things with it, when I heard a car arrive, up the avenue and across the gravel.

It stopped and the doors banged.

'Anyone home?' Manus's voice called, loudly.

CHAPTER THIRTEEN

Naomi was in the hallway, talking to my grandmother, when I got downstairs.

'Hi.' She gave me a cool nod.

'You got here early! And I see you've met my gr—'

'I *told* you we'd be here early! Don't you *ever* listen, Martha?'

Naomi is not an early riser. The journey down in the car with Manus had probably annoyed her as well.

'Pulled out of the wrong side of the bed this morning, were we?' I gave her a friendly jostle with my shoulder and she sniffed. 'Where's Man–' I began but she cut me short again.

'You've got a tan,' she accused. 'I thought you came down here to work.'

'I did. I do. But the hours are good. Plenty of time off.' I grinned at my grandmother. Her hair was tucked into the beret again and she was wearing one of her big aprons over a dress and jacket. It wasn't clear whether she was coming or going. She gave Naomi a nice friendly smile.

'The sun is a fringe benefit this summer,' she said. Naomi ignored her.

'And you've got fat,' she said to me.

'The food's good too.' I was curt. Being rude to me was one thing. Being rude to my grandmother was something else. I'd forgotten what a pain Naomi could be when she put her mind to it. Anyway, I hadn't put on *that* much weight. I hoped.

107

'Talking of food.' My grandmother turned to me briskly. 'I'm sure your friends would like something to eat, Martha. Just come down to the kitchen when you're ready.'

She called Fiachra, who'd been giving us the cold eye from the end of the stairs. He followed lazily, tail moving slowly. Touch of the morning grumbles there too, I thought.

'What a horrible cat,' Naomi said loudly. I'm sure my grandmother heard her.

'Oh, get a grip, Naomi!' I said. 'What's wrong with you? Look, I'm really glad you're here. It's great that you came, OK?' To show her I meant it I gave her a quick hug, even though she and I don't usually go in for that kind of thing. She sniffed. 'And you look great,' I added. That mollified her.

She did too, look great I mean. *She* had lost weight and was wearing a black mini skirt I hadn't seen before.

She nodded towards the door. 'You'd better say hello to Manus,' she said. But I'd already started toward the front door.

In the morning sun he looked devastatingly handsome. Even slightly unreal. But that was just a reflection of how distant I'd become from my life in Dublin. He was leaning against his mother's BMW, wearing shades and looking up at Lir House.

I stepped on to the gravel and he turned my way. He didn't move, just smiled. Behind me on the gravel I heard Naomi and swore silently. I'd hoped she would leave us alone at least while we said hello.

I stood in front of Manus and he took off the shades, grinning and looking me up and down.

'You got here early,' I said inanely.

'Couldn't keep away any longer.' He made no attempt to move from the car.

I nodded at the BMW. 'Looks like you're getting the adult treatment.'

'Yup.' He ran his hand along its side. 'I'm part of the family team now. I'll have my own wheels next year.' His eyes were very blue when he looked at me again. 'I like the tan,' he said. 'Suits you.' He put the shades back on and frowned up at Lir House. 'So this is Granny's pile? Looks to me as if it should have had its last season a long time ago.'

'Oh there's life in the old stones yet,' I laughed, forgiving him for not seeing how special Lir House was. I hadn't seen it myself at first. 'Anyway–' I waved a hand, 'just look at the location.' I meant this as a joke but Manus seemed to think I was serious.

'Location's fine, I'll grant you that. But the house is falling down. Needs a bundle spent on it.' He moved away from the car, took a longer view, 'I could get a really good deal on this place for Granny. With a little help from my old man, of course.'

'I don't know what my grandmother's plans are.' I spoke stiffly and he laughed.

'Sorry, Martha,' he said. 'Can't leave the job behind. That's my problem. Well, here I am, country girl. What're we going to do for the day?'

'Don't you want to bring your things into the house first?'

'We'll do that later,' Naomi stepped past me and opened the boot of the car. She hauled out a small bag. 'I feel sticky. I'd just love a swim.' She squinted at the sea. 'Where's this cove you wrote to me about?'

So the three of us went for a swim. We went straight away because Naomi said she found Lir House 'bloody morbid' and wouldn't even go back inside for my grandmother's food. I dropped into the kitchen and made an excuse but you could never fool my grandmother.

'Enjoy yourself.' She waved me away.

The water was just right. The morning chill had gone and it sparkled cool, green and clear. Just the way I had always imagined it would be when Manus and I shared our first swim there. Except that in my dream we'd always been alone.

As soon as I waded in Naomi joined me. I felt immediately guilty about not wanting her to be there. Manus mightn't be here at all if she hadn't persuaded him to come. 'God, this is good.' Naomi splashed herself and took off at a fast crawl. I floated out on my back, hoping Manus would join me. He did.

'Nice place you have here.' he trod water beside me. His hair glistened wet, his eyes shone, his skin gleamed. He was just perfect. He came closer.

'Glad you like it,' was all I managed to say. This was the moment, I was sure of it. He was going to kiss me, make my dream of so many nights come true. He bent over me.

And then Naomi, fairly zooming along, crashed into us.

The rest of the day was a bit like that. Three definitely *is* a crowd.

We drove into Wexford and moseyed around, went into a pub and listened to music. In another pub Manus played some pool until Naomi became bored and we left. Back in the car I told them about the fun-

fair and on the way back to Lir House, we stopped to
have a look at it.

'Well, Funderland it's not,' Naomi said. 'But I'm
willing to give it a whirl.' My own stomach turned
right over just seeing her look at the lethally high
Ferris wheel.

'I suppose there's electricity at your grandmother's
hotel? And running water?' Naomi giggled.

'Give it a rest, Naomi,' I said.

'Touchy, aren't we, about Granny and her house!
Have you noticed, Manus, how touchy our Martha is
about—'

'Leave it out, Naomi,' Manus snapped, as he started
the car again. I didn't need him to fight my battles but
it was nice to have him on my side. And the amazing
thing was that Naomi shut up. Just dropped the whole
thing.

We headed back to Lir House to clean up and eat.

It was sod's law, nothing else, that put Lorcan on the
road in front of us as we drove up the hill. He was
moving fast but he was, as usual, in the middle of the
road.

'What does that halfwit think he's doing?'

Before I could say anything Manus had blown the
horn, twice and loudly. Lorcan didn't move over. He
didn't look round either. I saw Manus's lips tighten as
he reached for the horn again.

'Don't!' I yelled. 'I know him. He's going to the
hotel.'

We were at the gates by then anyway. Lorcan turned
in and Manus, with a furious spurt of speed, overtook
him on the avenue.

I didn't look back. I couldn't.

'Who is he?' Naomi asked.

'My grandmother's chef.'

'Really? How *interesting!* A motorbike cook.' She giggled and I ground my teeth. 'Is he any good?'

'You can see for yourself. He'll be making dinner.'

Lorcan thundered past and came to a stop just as we were getting out of the car. It was impossible not to introduce him. He hung his helmet over the front of the bike as I went into the rigmarole about names, and nodded to Naomi and Manus in turn. I could tell he was annoyed about the horn-blowing.

'Martha says you're a chef.' Naomi's syes were all over him.

'That's right.'

Manus banged the door of the BMW. 'Hope you cook better than you ride that bike.'

'Nothing wrong with the way I—'

'Cut it out, you two.' I stepped between them, my heart hammering. I did *not* want this to happen. I took Lorcan by the arm. 'We're starving,' I said to him, then turned back to the others. 'Make yourselves at home in the drawing room while Lorcan and I get the food together.'

I was pretty pleased with the way I'd handled things and quite put out by Lorcan's bad mood in the kitchen. We worked in silence and, on my part, deep discomfort. When things were more or less prepared I left and went up to the drawing room.

Maurice, full of gallantry, was making conversation with a barely civil Naomi. My grandmother stood up, looked at me.

'Stay and keep your friends company,' she commanded. 'I'll help Lorcan tonight.'

Never have I obeyed anyone so readily.

Manus's food jokes began when my grandmother brought out the main course. It was a really good lasagne and Manus didn't seem to realise the jokes weren't appreciated. But at least he ate everything. Naomi didn't even try. I suppose not eating was how she lost all that weight.

The meal ended at last and I escaped by dragging Naomi up to my bedroom. She threw herself on the bed but almost immediately jumped up and began doing things to her eye make-up.

'Your French guest has certainly made himself at home, hasn't he?' she said.

'Mmm.'

I didn't explain Maurice to her. Not because I couldn't but because I found that I didn't want to. I was amazed by how much I didn't want to discuss with Naomi. Only six weeks before I'd been telling her everything that happened in my life. Now I didn't want to tell her anything at all about what had been happening in Lir House.

It wasn't just Naomi. It came to me that I didn't want to discuss it with anyone but Lorcan.

Not that Naomi would have heard me anyway. She was concentrating too hard on her eye make-up. Feeling I should make an effort for the night, and certainly not because I wanted to compete with her, I pulled on my denim mini skirt and a cropped T-shirt I'd bought in Wexford.

'Your hair's got long.' Naomi turned from the mirror. 'Why don't you do something with it?'

'Like?'

'Pile it up or something.'

I tried. It wasn't a howling success so I fixed a pair of hooped earrings onto my ears. It was the best I could so with the raw material.

'Help yourself.' Naomi threw a bottle of perfume my way. It was Poison, by Dior.

'Your mother's?' I asked.

'Mine now,' she said with a grin, snatching it back.

Manus was waiting for us in the car. We took off with enough spraying of gravel to send my grandmother on a terminal rampage. A good fifty per cent of it hit Lorcan's bike, still parked in its usual spot. I bit my lip as we careered down the avenue, trying not to think about how he'd feel. These were my friends, I reminded myself, come to see me. This was my night out with them. We were just having fun.

CHAPTER FOURTEEN

The fun-fair filled most of a large field outside the village. By the time we got there the air was pealing with screams and had a smell like candy floss stewed in hamburger. It being a Saturday night people had come from all over, most of them families with sunburnt children who whinged and wanted everything in sight. You couldn't blame them. There was a real hard sell going on in that field with rides, raffles and risks of one sort or another on offer everywhere.

We wandered through, considered the dodgems and the Ferris wheel, eyed the rifle range, left the swinging boats and carousel to the kids. A squeal from Naomi brought us to a halt by a terrifying thing called the Sirocco.

What was terrifying was its deathly simplicity. A rail line, narrow and fragile looking, climbed to the sky. At its highest point it looped, sickeningly, and plunged earthward again. Idiots stupid enough to buy trips on this contraption were carried aloft in an open, three-seater car.

'That's my thrill for the night!' Naomi danced about, clutching first at me and then Manus. I stared at her incredulously.

'Are you out of your tree?' I croaked. Just the sight of it was making my mouth dry up.

'Oh, stop behaving like an idiot!' Naomi turned and began pulling Manus toward the pay booth. 'You're not afraid, Manus, are you? You'll come with me.'

'Sure. My treat.'

I followed them on to the Sirocco. I sat in a daze as we were strapped into a car. I felt like a lemming, willingly following the others to my own, certain death. We left the ground and Manus, who was in the middle, leaned back and threw an arm around each of us. Naomi crossed her legs and gave a wild, giddy sort of laugh. The car began to gather speed and I closed my eyes.

'Open them!' Manus commanded in my ear. 'Stop copping out.'

And so, stupidly, I opened my eyes.

I saw Naomi's mouth, wide and yelling. I saw Manus's eyes, tense and glittering. I saw the sky rushing down to meet us as the car went howling upwards. My stomach turned right over and I closed my eyes, tight, just as we spun into the loop. But not before I saw trees, fields and screaming green take the place of the blue that had been the sky.

For a lifetime of seconds we hung, suspended and upside down. Then we were on the earthbound loop and I was a quivering jelly, a gibbering lump.

I sat on the grass, cradling my head against my knees and holding myself tightly together. Once they were sure I wasn't going to throw up or anything, Manus and Naomi went off to the Ferris wheel. Not for a million would I have gone with them. I couldn't even have faced the carousel.

'You feeling OK?'

When I managed to look up, Lorcan's face was looking down at me. He actually looked concerned.

The same could not be said of the female who clung

to his arm. Judy Moore glared. It was a look which said she'd be only too happy to see me keel over and die.

'I'm fine.' My voice was a squeak. I took a shuddering look at the Sirocco and was surprised to see it still functioning. 'I've come back from the dead but otherwise I'm fine.'

Lorcan looked as if he might have said something else but the lovely Judy pulled at him.

'You promised,' she hissed and Lorcan, with a last look in my direction, allowed himself be led away. He didn't even look back. I sniffed, gave my nose a good blow and stood up.

The Ferris wheel was turning. All of its cars were filled with whooping joy-riders. I squinted upwards, searching among them for Manus and Naomi. I saw them almost immediately, in a car on its way down and coming towards me.

They didn't see me. They were kissing, oblivious to the world and certainly to me, as their car whirled by and spun on, up into the air. I stayed, rooted where I was, until they came round again.

They were still kissing.

The wheel began to slow down but I didn't wait for it to stop.

For a while, walking through the fun-fair, I didn't feel anything. Lorcan had been right when he'd accused me of not noticing what went on around me. Why did things have to hit me between the eyes before I saw them? Manus and Naomi. Naomi and Manus. It had probably been going on since I left Dublin. Or before that for all I knew. What I couldn't figure out was why they'd bothered to come and visit me.

I stopped at a booth which had plastic ducks

circling in water. The object was to catch them as they went round. As I watched their aimless navigation my feelings began to function again. The loneliness was what hit me first. I had no one now. I didn't have Manus and I certainly didn't have a best friend any longer. I couldn't be said to have my grandmother since she had Maurice. Even Lorcan had abandoned me.

I tried not to think about Lorcan and how I'd treated him. He'd been a good friend, a really good friend, and I hadn't been straight with him about Manus.

But, what about Judy? Lorcan hadn't exactly been forthcoming about her himself.

Feelings of heartache and betrayal pretty well swamped me. I had trusted Naomi. I had trusted Manus. And they had used me. Both of them. I was a complete fool.

I took a fifty-pence piece from my pocket and practically threw it to the woman looking after the ducks. She gave me a hard look, which I ignored, and handed me a cue with a hook at the end. I began trapping her wretched ducks. It was a game for kids really but it gave me a certain, savage satisfaction when I won a panda bear. I felt that, for a change, I had got one over on someone.

I decided to go home, back to Lir House. I'd got as far as the edge of the field when Naomi's breathless cry sounded behind me. I clutched the panda tighter but didn't look back. I didn't even turn when she caught hold of my arm.

'Where're you going?' She actually had the gall to sound indignant. 'What's going on with you?' We've been looking everywhere.'

'Have you?' I was suddenly, scaldingly, angry. 'You weren't looking for me the last time I saw you. I was the last person in the world you wanted to see.'

I stopped, watching her face as the penny dropped. 'Oh, Martha.' At least she had the grace to bluster and blush. 'A kiss between friends. That's all it was. Surely you don't think...'

'Yes, I do think. I'm slow, Naomi, but I'm not on another planet. The signs were there, all day long, but I ignored them. You've worked hard to get Manus, haven't you? Well, now you've got him. And you're welcome to him. He's a lout, much more your type than mine.'

I didn't mean this. Not all of it anyway. It was pure temper speaking. Shouting more like. But somewhere, at the back of my mind, there was the feeling that it might be true. Or at least become true, tomorrow or the next day.

Naomi's eyes got darker and her face became smaller. That's what happens to her when she becomes angry. She is not a pretty sight.

'You're jealous!' she hissed. You never really had him and now you can't bear that he's mine...'

'Oh, be quiet, Naomi!' I really snarled. All I wanted right then was for her to sod off, take Manus with her.

But first I had to know something. I took a step closer, lowering the panda to my side. I'm a lot taller than Naomi and I was still hopping mad. She shut up. 'Why did you come down here together?' I demanded. 'Was it just to gloat?'

Her face took on a sulky look. She backed away before answering. For the first time in all the years I'd known Naomi I saw a spiteful look on her face. It was

119

a night of many awakenings.

'Manus wanted to come down. His father had heard something about Lir House and wanted him to have a look at it. But his mother wouldn't give him the car to drive this far on his own. So I offered to come with him. He said yes.' She shrugged, backed away another little bit. 'I went out with him a couple of times after you left. But that was just kind of friendly. Things kind of developed in the car on the way down. I can't help it if he likes me.'

I don't know what I would have said or done, if Manus hadn't come up just then. I'm sure he knew what was going on but it was obvious he intended to bluff things out. He was swaggering, full of bravado. He seemed to me almost a different person.

Before he could say anything I shoved the panda at him.

'A memento,' I said, 'of our brief and treacherous friendship. It was nice of you to drop by, Manus. I'll see you when I see you. And it *won't* be at the sale of my grandmother's house.'

He held the panda against him and looked at me stupidly. I really was noticing a lot of things tonight. Stupidity was not an expression I'd seen on Manus's face before. It looked quite natural there now.

'Oh, come *on*, Martha! What's wrong with you?'

Even his voice, now I listened properly, sounded different. Sort of whiney. 'Look, if it's because I had a bit of a whirl with Naomi.' He sniggered and my anger turned to the icy, enduring kind. 'Then forget it. That's over. It was just for a bit of a laugh anyway.'

He didn't even look at Naomi as he said this but I did. Under the tan her face had whitened. Her chin was wobbling and her eyes full of tears. I almost felt sorry for her. Manus put an arm around my shoulders and I froze. He didn't seem to notice.

'Look, Martha.' I recognised his house-selling voice.

'I've been thinking about you ever since you left town. I missed you.' He smiled. It was the crinkly, Manus smile of old

'Sod off, Manus.'

I said it quietly but with great force. And satisfaction. Even Manus, dim as I now knew him to be, saw that I meant it. He took his arm away. Naomi was crying quite openly.

'It's only an hour-and-half's drive to Dublin,' I said. 'You'll be home before midnight.' I had a stab of conscience. 'You can stay the night if you like,' I said to Naomi. 'There's a bed made up for you anyway. You can get a train home tomorrow.'

'You can keep your bed,' she said nastily.

Her tears were drying fast. The prospect of a drive through the night with Manus seemed to have cheered her up. I only hoped she knew what she was letting herself in for.

'If that's the way you want it.' Manus had dispensed with charm. 'I've spent enough time hanging around this kip anyway. Life among the rednecks has changed you, Martha. You're no fun any more. The yokels are welcome to you.'

He threw the panda at me, hard. I caught it as he turned heel and headed in the direction of the BMW. Naomi, without a word, tripped after him.

I was looking at the panda's sad, silly face when Manus called a last message.

'Hey Martha, old friend! I'm still Granny's best bet

when she comes to sell her hotel! Why don't you give her my telephone number?' He grinned the grin that would, I was sure, sell lots and lots of houses in the future. But not my grandmother's. Not Lir House.

I stood where I was until the crowd completely swallowed them up. I was still standing there when the BMW, horn blowing, sped past the field a few minutes later.

CHAPTER FIFTEEN

I walked home to Lir House. I walked slowly and, for a lot of the way, I cried. The warm air, the creeping dark, the high hedgerows along the road, all closed around me like a tunnel. I walked without seeing any light at its end.

I was feeling especially bad about Naomi. I had trusted her, absolutely. She had been my friend since we'd been eleven years old. Manus I'd never been sure of.

There were no lights on as I came up to the house and I thought Maurice and my grandmother must be in bed. But as I crunched miserably across the gravel I heard music and followed it to the drawing room window. They were both in there, sitting in the peace of the dying light, listening to something classical.

It wasn't my thing but I joined them anyway.

Neither of them asked me any questions. Maybe they knew the answers or maybe they were just being discreet. It could also have been that they were trusting me to handle things my way. I like to think that's what it was.

Whatever the reason they were right to leave me alone. It was while sitting there, with them, that I began to see light at the end of the tunnel.

I realised that my heart was intact. Manus had been right about one thing. My time in the country had changed me, though not in the way he seemed to think. It had helped me see things, especially him, differently.

This insight might have come to me anyway, even if he'd never tried to sell my grandmother's house while kissing my best friend. My mother would be *very* pleased. Distancing me from Manus had worked out better than she could possibly have hoped.

But distance had put my relationship with her in perspective too. It had given me knowledge and an unfair advantage. In some ways I now knew more about my mother than she did about me. For one thing, I knew that she had spent most of her life denying reality. I was not about to do the same thing.

In the week which followed my relationship with Lorcan changed, became careful. As the days went on this was the thing which bothered me most of all.

'Your friends didn't hang about then?' he asked me on Sunday evening. We were preparing dinner.

'No,' I said, and the conversation ended. I didn't want to talk about Naomi and Manus. I *did* want to talk about Judy Moore but didn't see how I dared. I wanted to know if he'd taken her to the fair or had just met her there.

It was none of my business of course. And if there had ever been a chance of it being my business I'd blown it by not coming straight about Manus. I hadn't treated Lorcan the way a friend should, and he knew it. He became cautious with me, watchful of what he said. I missed the easy fun, the trust we'd had. And I missed the swims.

It was August now and the weather more fitful. Maurice gave me painting lessons and my grandmother sat with us while I attempted sea and landscapes.One day I even painted the pair of them. We laughed a lot at the result.

Maurice took occasional taxi trips, which he didn't discuss. I figured he was either having secret manicures or buying paint and paper so I didn't probe. But for the most part the three of us spent our time around the house and garden, not doing anything much, avoiding the fast-approaching realities of September.

We never spoke about what was going to happen to Lir House or about where my grandmother was going to live. Maurice's return to France was never discussed and the issue of whether or not I would go back to school might not have existed. Most deeply buried was the problem of how we were going to present my mother with her 'dead father'.

'We are making memories,' my grandmother said to me one day. I knew exactly what she meant.

She and Maurice took to talking to me about the summer of 1946.

It was like listening in on another world and I never once found it boring. 'That summer,' Maurice said one day, 'people really began to put the war behind them. It was as if the world had ended and was beginning again. Everyone believed there would be peace for ever. They didn't believe this for long, of course. Only until another atom bomb was dropped over the Bikini atoll in the Pacific.'

'The radioactive cloud could be seen ten miles away but the palm trees still stood.'

'We were hardly aware of it here, though.' My grandmother always brought things back to the basics of Lir House. 'The weather was so good that summer.

Thirteen hours of sunshine were recorded one day in July.'

Maurice was easily deflected. 'And in August you locked the hotel for three days while we went to the Horse Show in Dublin.'

'I did—at the height of the season too. I turned away bookings, I remember. But it was worth it. The Show was a carnival that year.'

'The silk dresses and ostrich-feather chapeaux! Le *Capitaine Fresson*, on his magnificant Jacynthe, giving the best performance in the Aga Khan trophy.'

At this my grandmother gave a throaty guffaw which ended in a fit of coughing. When she got her breath back she tapped a slightly peeved looking Maurice on the arm. 'But Ireland defeated France for the overall trophy. Don't you remember that?'

'Of course,' Maurice shrugged. 'Ireland did well. But le *Capitaine Fresson!*'

My grandmother laughed again, more restrainedly this time. 'You have never forgiven your team for not winning that trophy, have you Maurice?'

'No.' Maurice was emphatic and quite disgruntled looking.

Another day, as I sat watching him paint, Maurice gave a long sigh and said, 'H.G.Wells died that year also.' The name meant nothing to me, then, and I was afraid to say anything in case Maurice was talking about a personal loss. Realising the depths of my ignorance he went on to more mundane matters. 'I bought a grey hat with a silk band in Dublin for eleven shillings and nine pence,' he said.'I have it still.'

My grandmother, arriving with cold drinks, picked up the end of his reminiscing. 'That same day–' She handed the orange round. '–we had a four-course lunch for two shillings and went to the Metropole cinema to see Margaret Lockwood and Vic Oliver in *I'll Be Your Sweetheart*.'

'But there were no cigarettes.' Maurice pulled a face. 'We could not get any because of a strike in Dublin docks. You were not pleased.'

One afternoon, when Maurice began to talk again about the ostrich-feather hats and silk dresses worn by the women at the Horse Show, I asked my grandmother if she had ever dressed like that.

'I certainly did,' she said. 'I've kept a lot of my finery too. Come upstairs and I'll show you.' In her room she opened a chest. It was deep, reeked of her perfume and was filled with clothes worth killing for. 'Have fun,' she said and left me there.

I lifted out dress after dress in silk and rayon, clunky sling-backed shoes and, most glorous of all, a pale green ostrich-feathered hat. She hadn't said not to so I tried things on. The dresses were tight but I got into them, just about, and the shoes were a reasonable fit too. But the hat was perfect. Not to be worn to your average disco but just the thing for a touch of the light fantastic.

I liked myself so much in one particular silk dress— red with green spots, a cross-over bodice, short sleeves and two pleats—that I ran down to ask Maurice to take my photo. I sashayed across the lawn, balancing the ostrich feathers on my head. The effect on Maurice was gratifying. He stood up, spread his arms wide and cried, '*Ravissant!*'

This went to my head and I fooled around for a bit, doing a catwalk routine. My grandmother clapped her hands. 'Keep the dress,' she cried, 'and the hat. In fact you may take the whole trunk with you!'

I protested, feebly, as she insisted. When I gave her a grateful hug she went stiff with embarrassment. Maurice filled the awkward moment. 'I will paint you like that,' he announced.

He did too. It took him two days and it's a lovely picture. In it I am smiling, almost a lady and quite the *ingénue*. If he'd painted it a week later I sure I would have looked a lot different. By then I'd begun to learn something about life.

In as much as we ever learn anything about life.

The learning process began three days later, when we were walking in the garden and my grandmother collapsed.

CHAPTER SIXTEEN

My grandmother had cancer. She had known she was ill for a long time but the disease had stopped its advance and she'd hoped to get that summer, and maybe even another winter, of life. It didn't happen that way.

Maurice had known since the night of the storm. She had begun to feel ill again and had told him as they sat together in the kitchen. Even then she had hoped to survive the summer. She thought she could surmount anything.

Maurice told me all of this the afternoon she collapsed. He was very capable when it happened, but then he wasn't half as shocked as I was. He dropped immediately to her side, lifting her head and cradling it gently. I gaped like an idiot, not knowing what to do.

'Go to your grandmother's room!' He looked up and spoke to me so sharply that I jumped. 'Beside her bed you will find two bottles of tablets. Bring the blue ones. Quickly.'

My grandmother stirred. As she opened her eyes he bent and said something I couldn't hear. She didn't reply but her eyes never left his. He looked up at me again.

'Please, Martha! Go quickly and get the tablets.' I went.

Half an hour later we had my grandmother in bed. Willpower and the tablets had helped her climb the stairs with only a little assistance. Maurice and I left as she dozed off.

'What's wrong with her?' I asked the question shakily, hoping Maurice would say it was nothing to worry about.

Knowing he wouldn't.

I had never been faced with illness before. Never once could I remember my mother being seriously ill, my father either. It had terrified me, seeing my grandmother change to a grey-white, barely breathing creature before my eyes.

Maurice told me everything, gently but matter-of-factly.

'She is dying,' he said. 'And she is doing it as she has done everything else in her life, in her own way, in her own home. We must help her, *ma chère*, you and I.'

He became a blur in front of my eyes. The blur moved, pulled out a chair and put me sitting by the table. It handed me a handerchief and let me get on with a good cry.

'It's not fair,' I said at last.

'No, *ma chère*, it is not fair. Life is not fair...'

Maurice made us coffee and we sat there for an hour or more, sometimes talking, sometimes not. He went up to check on my grandmother once, but she was still asleep. When he came down I asked him why he hadn't told me before that she was ill.

'What was the point?' he asked. 'She wanted you to have a perfect summer, to enjoy this place at least once before she went. She did not want you to remember her as a dying old woman. You must not be angry with her.'

I shook my head. After a while I managed to speak again. 'Of course I'm not angry with her.'

'Maybe...' Maurice spoke slowly and I could see how tired he was. '...it would have been better if you had not come to know her. If things had stayed as they were. Now you will have the pain of grief.

'How can you say that?' I felt desolate and angry all at once. 'Getting to know her has been once of the best things that's happened to me.'

It was true. My grandmother, by taking me into her life, had helped me sort out so much of my own. Just having known her would go *on* helping me. And oh, how I would grieve for her.

Maurice explained about his taxi trips too. My grandmother had not wanted to make any more visits to the hospital, or to her doctor. There was nothing either could do for her anyway. Not now. So Maurice had undertaken to collect her perscribed medicine and painkillers.

'Oh, Maurice.' I reached for his hand and held it for a while, thinking about the summer and all the things I hadn't known.

The sound of a motorbike on the gravel outside made me think of something else. 'I'll tell Lorcan,' I said.

Maurice patted my hand and let it go. 'And I will go to Martha,' he said.

He left and I started to get the kitchen ready for Lorcan. I was ready myself to take on whatever I would have to do for the rest of the summer. Playtime was over, I knew that. From now on, and I didn't care how long it took, I would look after my grandmother. Along with Maurice.

I hoped I would be up to whatever lay ahead.

SEVENTEEN

The days got shorter. But not cooler. The hot weather returned for the last two weeks of August, cruelly sunny this time. The air seemed to stand still.

But not my grandmother's cancer.

The periods when she was well became fewer, the times when she was weak and ill went on longer. She never complained and she would not be hospitalised. It was never even up for discussion. Sick or well she dressed every morning, came down to breakfast. Her way of dressing didn't change either. She was cluttered as ever and, though it must have caused her painful effort, she still put her hair up with combs every day.

But she hardly ate at all. That, in someone who had taken such joy in food, was one of the things which frightened me most. She sat to dinner each evening, talking and listening to Maurice and me as if nothing had happened, as if she weren't failing before our eyes. I had to remind myself that she wasn't immortal, that she only gave that impression.

Maurice was determinedly cheerful and I took my cue from him.

It was my grandmother who decided we should postpone telling my mother about her illness. 'It may not come for a long time yet,' she said one morning.

She meant her death. It was the first time she had directly referred to it and I had to look away. She touched my hand, gently. I still couldn't look at her.

'We're having such a lovely time together, you,

Maurice and I. 'Her voice was hoarse. It often was in the mornings. 'I want us to have a little bit longer...Jane and I have been separate for so long. She'll be upset. And there will be such a lot of explaining to do. Anyway,' she coughed and her voice came out stronger, 'I may have another remission and live to be a hundred. And then where would we be? All the fuss would have been for nothing.'

We didn't argue with her, Maurice and I. It was her life. And it was her death. But we didn't for a minute think she would get better.

So we didn't tell my mother. Not then anyway.

I told Lorcan what the score was the day after her collapse. He didn't say anything for a long time. We were in the kitchen and he was cleaning fish. I'd tried to tell him before we started on the job but couldn't. As it was I blurted it out and then stood there feeling terrible when he said nothing. He just went on gutting the fish. After a while, trying not to cry, I started to tell him again. He stopped me with a sort of grunt.

'It's all right, Martha,' he said at last. 'I heard you. I thought there was something wrong. I never thought of...cancer.'

He went on with the fish. I got him a bucket for the guts and we kept ourselves busy for a while, saying nothing.

'It's not fair, is it?' he said when we'd finished.

'No. Not a bloody bit fair,' I said.

Fiachra, smelling of fish, hovered ingratiatingly. I fed him the offal in the back garden and sneaked a look through the window at Lorcan. He was drying his hands and looking into space. He wasn't crying exactly.

I went into the kitchen and stood in front of him. When he looked at me I said, 'She was happy this summer.'

I gave him a hug and he held me for a minute.

We had the dinner practically ready when my grandmother came into the kitchen.

'Well, Lorcan, what're we having tonight?' she demanded.

'Baked trout,' Lorcan said. 'Would you prefer something else?'

'Trout's lovely.' She began lifting the lids off pots and generally poking around. She was skeletal now, a stick woman with arms and legs like the branches on a winter tree. But she'd caught her hair back in the pearly combs and had, still, something of what Maurice called her *'savoir faire'*.

Inspection over, she handed Lorcan an envelope she'd been holding in her hand. 'You'll need this reference for the people in the Alps...'

'Thanks.' Lorcan took the envelope, looked at it, turned it over. 'Thanks for everything.' He kept his head down.

'Oh, come on now! It says nothing but good things. All of them true.' My grandmother gave one of her deep chortles. 'You'll make a fine chef, Lorcan. When are you off?'

'The third of September.' He stuffed the envelope into his pocket.

His answer was a shock to me. Switzerland was not on my list of places to visit and I was unlikely to be coming back to Lir House. I might not see him again.

'So soon!' My grandmother echoed what I was thinking. 'We must have a farewell dinner then, before you go. You will be the guest and Martha, Maurice and I will do everything...'

She left the kitchen quite pleased with herself. Lorcan and I felt better too. Which I'm sure is what she intended.

We didn't get to have the dinner. My grandmother became ever weaker and spent more and more time in bed. Maurice and I took turns sitting with her. Poor Maurice seemed to shrink during that time. He read to her a lot, in French. I'm not sure if she understood but she certainly liked to listen to him.

And Fiachra disappeared. One day he was there and the next I couldn't find him anywhere. I didn't want to tell my grandmother but she knew anyway. She asked for him and shook her head when I tried to pretend he was off hunting in the garden.

'It's all right, Martha,' she said. 'I thought he'd be off one of these days. He's gone to find another home. He has to look out for himself, you know. Cats do.' She smiled. 'Especially toms. I'm glad. I don't need to worry about him now.'

The doctor came daily, the same nice, hearty man who'd come before. One day he spent longer than usual with her and, when he came downstairs, he said yes to a glass of Maurice's wine. 'She was never a one to ask for a visit unless she really needed something.' He looked reflectively into his glass. His round face was sad. 'The disease was well advanced before she ever came to see me, you know. She knew what it was, said she knew there wasn't much I could do about curing it. There's such a thing as being too independent.'

He took a long swig of his wine. 'To be frank, I

thought her remission would last longer. Even when the cancer became active again I thought it would progress more slowly than it has.' He sighed heavily. 'I'm afraid you'll need to get a nurse in to help very soon. I'll arrange that for you.' He finished his wine in a gulp, looked from one of us to the other. 'I realise there are problems involved, and that Martha herself is the stumbling block, but it is time her daughter was told.'

And so the decision to tell my mother was taken.

My grandmother told her herself. She telephoned that very evening. There really wasn't any other way to do it. Maurice and I settled her by the phone and then moved off. When a mother has to tell her daughter that she's dying she doesn't need an audience.

She was quite a long time on the phone. Afterwards she told us that my parents would be arriving at the weekend. She was tired so I didn't try to get her to talk any more about it. But I wondered how my mother was feeling. I thought about phoning her but was too caught up in everything. I couldn't think what I would say anyway. But I should have made time and I should have tried to find the words. I know that now.

The next day a miraculous breeze blew up and my grandmother announced that she was feeling much better. She looked it too. Her skin had lost some of its pallor and her eyes were nearly clear. Maurice became quite excited and said he would organise a treat.

Maurice was very good at that kind of thing. He hired an open-topped car and insisted that my grandmother and I put on our best gear. Then he drove us on a sort of grand tour, slowly out along the coast road, through the village and along a windy, tree-lined road. The summer was definitely turning and the colours everywhere were becoming older and deeper.

We had afternoon tea in a posh hotel where my grandmother delighted in finding fault with as many things as possible. We stayed until she said she wanted to go. Maurice put the hood up then and drove us home.

Later, I watched from my room as he and my grandmother walked slowly down the path to the cliff. They didn't go very far. I suppose it was because my grandmother became tired. Maurice put an arm around her and they turned back.

It was the last time they walked together.

My grandmother did not get up the next morning and we send for the nurse.

CHAPTER EIGHTEEN

My mother arrived just before my grandmother died on Friday night.

Maurice and I were sitting on each side of the bed when she came into the room. Maurice stood up, very politely, but she hardly noticed him. Poor Maurice.

My father stood just inside the door. He didn't seem to know what else to do.

The nurse had explained things to my mother on the way up the stairs. Even so, I could see that she was really shocked by my grandmother's appearance. She had become a wraith. I had combed her hair and put the pearly combs into it but nothing made much difference now. She was a woman waiting for death, her breathing hardly there.

My mother gave a small cry and fell to her knees beside the bed. She took one of the white hands in her own.

'Mother?'

My grandmother opened her eyes.

'Jane, my child...'

That was all she said and it was the last thing she said. I really believe that she waited until my mother arrived to die.

My mother stayed on her knees and cried. I stood behind her and put my hand on her head. Someone was going to have to help her face things. Maurice could not be denied, nor my grandmother's life and choices ignored. My mother's hair, under my hand, was very soft. She leaned against me, still crying.

We stayed that way for a long time, watching with Maurice as life quietly left my grandmother.

CAVAN COUNTY LIBRARY

Attic Press hopes you enjoyed **Goodbye, Summer, Goodbye**. To help us improve the **Bright Sparks** series for you please answer the following questions.

1. Why did you decide to buy this book?

_____

_____

_____

2. Did you enjoy this book? Why?

_____

_____

_____

3. Where did you buy it?

_____

_____

_____

4. What do you think of the cover?

_____

_____

_____

4. Have you ever read any other books in the BRIGHT SPARKS series? Which one/s?

_____

_____

_____

If there is not enough space for your answers on this coupon continue on a sheet of paper and attach it to the coupon.

Post this coupon to **Attic Press**, 4 Upper Mount Street, Dublin 2 and we'll send you a **BRIGHT SPARKS** bookmark.

Name _____

Address _____

_____

You can order your books by post, fax and phone direct from:
Attic Press, 4 Upper Mount St, Dublin 2. Ireland.
Tel: (01) 66 16 128 Fax: (01) 66 16 176

GOODBYE, SUMMER, GOODBYE

Class No. _____ J _____   Acc No. C|53762

Author: Doyle, R   Loc: // SEP 1995

**LEABHARLANN
CHONDAE AN CHABHAIN**

1. **This book may be kept three weeks. It is to be returned on / before the last date stamped below.**
2. **A fine of 20p will be charged for every week or part of week a book is overdue.**

// JAN 2003

© Rose Doyle 1994

All rights reserved. Except for brief passages quoted in newspaper, magazine, radio or television reviews, no part of this book may be reproduced in any form or by any means, electronic or mechanical, including photocopying or recording, or by any information storage and retrieval systems without prior permission from the Publishers.

First published in Ireland in 1994 by
Attic Press
4 Upper Mount Street
Dublin 2

A catalogue record for this title is available from the British Library

ISBN 1 85940 434

The moral right of Rose Doyle to be identified as the author of this work is asserted.

Cover Design: Angela Clarke
Origination: Verbatim Typesetting and Design
Printing: The Guernsey Press Co Ltd.

This book is published with the assistance of The Arts Council/An Chomhairle Ealaíon.

1 1 JAN 2003

CAVAN COUNTY LIBRARY
ACC. No. .... C/ 53763
CLASS No. .... J(1)
INVOICE NO. 2.957
PRICE .... £ 4.99

Cavan County Library
Withdrawn Stock